Habitat

stories of *BENT* realism

Books by Walter Cummins

Story Collections
Habitat: stories of BENT realism
The Lost Ones
The End of the Circle
Local Music
Where We Live
Witness

Novels
A Stranger to the Deed
Into Temptation

Nonfiction
The Literary Traveler, with Thomas E. Kennedy
Programming Our Lives: Television and American Identity,
with George Gordon
Managing Management Climate, with George Gordon
Florham: The Lives of an American Estate,
with Carol Bere and Samuel Convissor

Edited
Writers on the Job, with Thomas E. Kennedy
Shifting Borders: East European Poetry of the Eighties
The Other Side of Reality: Myths, Vision & Fantasies,
with Martin Green and Margaret Verhulst

www.waltercummins.com

Habitat

stories of *BENT* realism

Walter Cummins

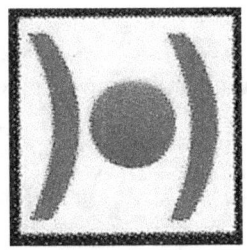

Del Sol Press
Washington, D.C.

Habitat:
stories of *BENT* realism
by Walter Cummins

Published by Del Sol Press
Washington, D.C.

First printing 2013

Cover photo: Walter Cummins, Boughton, Kent, 1980

Printed in the United States of America

ISBN 978-0615850108

Thanks to Alison Cummins and Renée Ashley for thorough and perceptive editing.

for

all the survivors and all those who did their best

Acknowledgments

The stories in this collection first appeared in the following publications:

"Habitat" in *South Carolina Review*
"Miss Wilcox's Ghost" in *St. Andrews Review*
"Call Her" in *Molossus*
"In the Old Village" in *Tiferet*
"The Peacock in the Garden" in *Laurel Review*
"Queen's Palace" in *Berkeley Poets Cooperative*
"Black Hole" in *Outerbridge*, reprinted in *Redux*
"Evan in the Tent" in *Contrary*
"In the Woods" in *New Madrid*
"Gypsies" in *Anathema Review*
"Cigarettes" in *Kiosk*
"Tobar's Journey" in *Del Sol Review*
"Goggles" in *3rd Bed*
"Vérité" in *The MacGuffin*
"Oubliette" in *Contemporary World Literature*, reprinted in
    Serving House: A Journal of Literary Arts
"Removal" in *Conspire*
"The Prince of Sixth Street" in *Perigee*
"His Mother's Child" in *The Girl with Red Hair*
"Steinway and the Wizard" in *Conspire*
"Reverse" in *Rain Dog Review*
"Under the Deck" in *Princeton Arts Review*
"Structure" in *Abiko Quarterly*

Contents

Habitat / 9

Miss Wilcox's Ghost / 19

Call Her / 28

In the Old Village / 44

The Peacock in the Garden / 47

Queen's Palace / 55

Black Hole / 61

Evan in the Tent / 73

In the Woods / 80

Gypsies / 92

Cigarettes / 97

Tobar's Journey / 100

Goggles / 110

Vérité / 113

Oubliette / 126

Removal / 136

The Prince of Sixth Street / 141

His Mother's Child / 148

Steinway and the Wizard / 153

Reverse / 156

Under the Deck / 165

Structure / 178

HABITAT

Paul was happy when mother and father chose the apartment on their first afternoon of visiting the newspaper rental listings. Father, bearing a certified check, went back the next morning to sign the lease with the landlord who lived in the apartment downstairs and told them to call him Mr. A. Father felt pleased with himself for talking Mr. A into a two-year term at a rent they could afford.

Grandma wanted to know all about the closets, Great Aunt Edna about the bathroom, older sister Martha about the southern exposure. They were all pleased by what they heard. The apartment sounded perfect, especially for so many people. Mother and Father would have the bedroom off the dining area, Grandma and Great Aunt Edna the master bedroom, Martha and little sister Grace the narrow bedroom over the stairwell, and Paul and his brother Robert what had been a storage pantry next to the kitchen.

With only space for a bunk bed, the brothers had to stack their clothing on built-in shelves that smelled of garlic, but they didn't object. In their last apartment they slept in the dining area on canvas Army cots that had to be set up each evening, while Martha and Grace used the sofa bed in the living room. Mother was always finding stray socks and undergarments behind the chairs and lamp tables but tried not to complain, even though Grandma was a compulsively neat woman.

Here in the new apartment they could, at least in pairs, shut a door and have a few hours privacy. Paul could hide his secret magazines on the highest of his shelves under winter sweaters. Great Aunt Edna could slip into the bathroom in the middle of the night without awakening half the family with her hollow old woman's noises.

On the first relaxed evening, after the week it took to unpack the boxes, hang the curtains, and lay the carpets, they lingered at the dinner table with extra cups of coffee and bottles of soda pop to debate which feature of the apartment was the very best. Great Aunt Edna claimed the water pressure, Robert the plexiglass shower door, Mother the self-cleaning oven, Grace the TV reception, Grandma the linen closet, Father the dimming light switches, Martha the strong sunlight that poured through the front windows, and Paul—embarrassed by the frivolity of his choice—the floral wallpaper. The competition was merely a game, good-natured, each pleased with the others' favorites.

Mr. A visited occasionally when they first moved in, always using the back stairs and rapping at the hallway door beside the linen closet. He was a small man with a large head, the cheeks and jaw even more disproportioned, as if swollen from a toothache. He wore starched white shirts with pointed collars and sleeves precisely folded to the elbows. His voice grated with hoarseness and he spoke slowly, as if English were not natural to him, yet revealed no sign of an accent.

The family members kept remarking to each other what a pleasant man he was, though Paul did not tell anyone, not even Robert, that it made him queasy to look at the man's bloated face, the grey pallor of his flesh.

Mother invited Mr. A to bring his wife for a visit so that they all could meet her. He smiled so broadly they could see the clamps of his bridgework. "In time," he said. "In time."

Mr. A did not appear again for two weeks. Father waited past the first of the month expecting him to collect the rent check, but finally slipped it into the lower mailbox. Great Aunt Edna, just emerging from the bathroom, was the one who felt his footsteps vibrating on the back stairway. She hissed to Mother and Martha, and the family was already gathered around the door before he rapped.

He looked sheepish when Mother slipped the bolt and opened it. "I'm afraid I have to ask you for a favor," he said.

"Yes?"

"These houses were built before television, even before radio. The sound carries terribly. Downstairs your programs seem to blast through the walls. In every room."

"We'll make it quieter," Father promised.

"But Great Aunt Edna is hard of hearing," Martha said, touching the old woman's shoulder.

"I'm afraid turning it down won't help," Mr. A said. "The last family tried that. The sound still penetrates."

"What do you want us to do?" Robert asked.

"Would you turn your set off at nine-thirty?"

"Do you and Mrs. A go to sleep that early?" Mother said.

"I'm afraid we do."

"But all the good programs are on then!" Grace wailed when he was gone.

Paul thought of a compromise that they tried for several nights. The television set had an earphone jack that bypassed the speaker. One of them would listen through the tiny ear button and whisper to the others a summary of what was being said. But the method became aggravating. Their comprehension lagged behind the action on the screen and Great Aunt Edna sulked because she could not hear the whispering. One night she got so angry she stood right in front of the set with her black skirt pulled wide, blocking the picture for everyone. Mother, who hated discord, stood up and said, "That's it. That's enough. The set goes off at nine-thirty."

They tried other activities—card games, puzzles, baking, sewing. But most of the family members began to drift off to separate rooms soon after the screen went blank.

A few days before the next month's rent was due, Mr. A rapped again. Paul let him in and felt chill at the grey expression on the man's face. The others were seated at the dining table, staring up over empty plates. Only Great Aunt Edna, who had not heard, scraped a spoon across the bottom of her pudding bowl. Mother offered a cup of coffee, but Mr. A declined.

"You've all been so cooperative," he said, cleaning his rimless glasses with the tip of his tie and not looking at any one of them. "I hate to ask for another favor."

"What is it?" Martha's hand clenched a teaspoon.

"You're all such early risers." Mr. A tried to smile but just stood over them with his lips parted.

"That's because there's nothing for us to stay up for," Grace said.

Grandma pinched her arm.

"You're all up by five-thirty," Mr. A said.

"My sons have to leave for work by a quarter to seven," Mother told him. Paul and Robert supported the family. Grandma had social security and Father drew a small pension. Martha could never find a job where they appreciated her. But, of course, Mother revealed none of that to Mr. A. The family's finances were its own concern.

"I appreciate that they have to work," Mr. A said.

"Then what are you asking us to do?" Father said.

"The main problems are the footsteps and the showers. The floor squeaks and the ceiling thumps. And these pipes are so old the water pumping through them makes a terrible noise in the downstairs walls. Like cats screaming."

"Maybe you should replace the pipes," Martha said.

"Out of the question. It would mean a major renovation. I have two small requests. That you don't put on shoes until you are about to leave the house and that you take your showers in the evening."

Father traced his pinky about the edge of his saucer.

"My sons' showers are very important to them," Mother said.

"They might be even more refreshing after a hard day's work." Mr. A rubbed his knuckles.

"I'm a bit confused," Martha told him despite Grandma's frowns. "I thought you went to bed at nine-thirty. How can you sleep past six?"

Mr. A gave one of his infrequent grins. "I suppose we're not like you."

As soon as he closed the door, Grace ran to her room and threw herself on the bed in a tantrum. But Mother scolded her for such a childish reaction. "You just have to accept these things." Father, Grandma, and Great Aunt Edna nodded in unison.

Paul suggested that it would help matters if Mother got to know Mrs. A; they might even become friends. Mother brightened and pinched his cheek the way she had done when he was a child. The next few days, morning, afternoon, and evening, she called the A's number in hopes of introducing herself to the woman they still had not met. But Mr. A always answered the phone and said his wife couldn't speak at the moment.

Out of curiosity, Martha and Grace began to watch at the windows for Mrs. A, Martha in the front from the living room, Grace from the kitchen. For days they saw no one except Mr. A's arms reaching for the newspapers on the front steps. But Grace one day called out, "I just saw him! Dragging a big bundle into the garage."

Martha hurried into the kitchen, arriving at the window in time to see Mr. A close the garage door. She quickly dialed his number in hopes of catching Mrs. A alone. But on the very first ring Mr. A answered.

Grace began to cry. Mother comforted her with an embrace. "He must have an extension in the garage."

Soon afterwards, one night at ten, Grandma and Great Aunt Edna already asleep, Martha tweezing her eyebrows at the bathroom mirror, Paul and Robert sharing a peanut butter snack in the kitchen, Mr. A banged on the door with what sounded like both fists. Father answered, but—without a greeting—Mr. A demanded to see Mother. She came out of her room in a pink quilted robe and fuzzy pink slippers, her face white with cold cream. "What is it?"

"There are clothespins all over the yard." Mr. A glowered.

"We hang clothes from the kitchen window." Mother was speaking calmly although Paul could see her right hand trembling behind her back. "Sometimes the pins fall off the pulley line or slip out of my fingers."

"They must be picked up."

"I'll do it first thing in the morning."

"No. Now. At once!"

"It's pitch dark."

Mr. A pulled a very long, eight-battery flashlight from his jacket and shined it in her face.

By now Martha's head, red hair disheveled, appeared at the opening of the bathroom door. "Don't do it, Mother," she pleaded.

But Mother shrugged toward Father, sighed, and followed Mr. A down the stairs.

Paul, Robert, and Father grouped at the window to watch Mother's hands reach into the circles cast by Mr. A's flashlight and gather the scattered clothespins. In the silence they heard Martha snap "Shut up!"

at Great Aunt Edna but did not turn their heads.

Within a week the leaves fell from the two small trees in the yard and the cold weather set in. The radiators began hissing at once. "Well, at least he's giving us plenty of heat," Grandma said. But the next day they realized too much heat was coming up. The valves shrilled a continuous whistle and damp steam clouded the apartment. Robert brought home a thermometer that registered ninety-four degrees.

Mother reminded them that they had promised in their lease not to open the windows when the furnace was working. So the young people, even Father, walked around in shorts, their bodies slick with sweat. But when Great Aunt Edna, a frail old woman, fainted, Robert threw open windows in all the rooms.

Five minutes later the phone rang. Father answered. Even before he could say hello, Mr. A began ranting. "I pay good money to heat this house. And you think nothing of squandering it. I don't know why I should give people like you any heat at all." He spoke so loudly everyone in the family could hear.

"But it's like living in a steam bath," Father said.

"Heat rises. We must have it at least eighty-five down here."

"But we can't take it." Father's voice quavered and his face began to flush purple.

"I hate waste! Close the windows or you'll get no heat at all."

The family, which never disagreed, which rarely spoke in raised tones, argued loudly. Robert didn't care if they had any heat. Grandma feared the real cold of winter and thought it might not be so bad once the outside temperature fell. Martha screamed that she hated living there. Finally, Mother pounded her fist on the table and declared, "I won't stand for this!" She stomped from room to room slamming windows and snapping their locks.

The next day Robert set up fans in the living room and dining area, and the temperature dropped to eighty-seven on his thermometer.

On Saturday evening Grace found a special delivery letter in the mailbox. It was from Mr. A, notarized, announcing that, because they were wasting so much water and electricity, he was limiting their supply. Water from eight till nine a.m. and six to seven p.m. Electricity the same hours, except for an evening extension from nine to nine-thirty.

"Why didn't he come up to tell us himself?" Grandma asked, clucking her tongue. "Or call?" Great Aunt Edna added.

"It's illegal!" Martha shouted. "I know that much about the law. Our lease says he supplies electricity and water." She had taken to reading the lease again and again through the day.

"Martha's right," Robert said. Paul nodded.

"What should we do?" Father asked.

"Go to the police," Robert suggested.

"Now!" Martha insisted.

"No. Wait until morning," Mother said. "Let's all get a good night's sleep to prepare ourselves."

Martha was dressed at six the next morning. But Robert wanted a shower before they went to the municipal building, and since the water did not come on until eight, was not ready until eight-thirty.

When Martha, Robert, and Paul stepped toward the door, Mother blocked their path. "No! I've changed my mind. This family has never had doings with the police before. We've always taken care of our own problems."

"I hate that man!" Martha sank to the floor between Robert and Paul, shaking with sobs.

"But Mother," Robert pleaded. Paul turned at once to dial Mr. A's number, willing to beg for consideration. The phone rang twelve times before someone lifted it and immediately broke the connection. The same thing happened the next three times he called.

Martha stormed downstairs to slam her pocketbook against the A's door then kicked at the lower panel. She cursed and hobbled back up with a swollen toe, swearing it was broken.

Robert made Paul pledge that the two of them would stay home from work until Mr. A gave them satisfaction. Father was furious when they told him. "You bastards! You know I can't live on my pension." When Robert tried to explain, Father spit on the carpet at his feet.

Mother began to cry.

"What if he makes us move?" Grandma said. "Where would we

go?"

"It doesn't matter!" Martha cried. "This place is awful!"

"And what else could we afford? Tiny rooms? I'd rather be dead than live that way again. Wouldn't you, Edna?"

The old woman nodded over and over, gumming the flesh inside her cheeks.

"You're all cowards!" Martha rushed into the kitchen to hurl pots down against the floor, resounding sharp metal clanking throughout the house, ignoring Mother's demands that she stop.

Father shoved Robert toward her. "Grab your sister! Hold her arms!"

Paul found himself disagreeing. "Let her do it. It has to be done."

Father began punching him on the back. "I'm your father, damn you!"

Robert reached out toward Martha and she kicked at him, threatened with a skillet. Grace tried to throw herself between them. They were all shouting and shrieking, the whole family, even Great Aunt Edna. At the phone's single ring they froze in silence.

"It's him," Paul said. But, when he stepped toward it, the ringing stopped.

Martha broke from the kitchen, pulled Grace into their room, and slammed the door. Father twisted Paul's ear until his knees buckled from the pain. "See what you've done," Father hissed. But Paul had no idea what he meant. Mother passed alone into her room, Grandma into hers, Great Aunt Edna into the bathroom.

By the middle of the night Robert's thermometer read one hundred and six degrees. He had to light a match to see it with the electricity off. Paul whispered that he must get outside to breathe. But, after he groped through the darkness, he found both the front and back door locks jammed as if rusted solid. When Robert tried to push open the windows, they stuck after moving only a few inches. From behind Martha's door came a crashing of glass. The others crowded into the hallway, bumping and shoving because they could not see. But Martha would not open for them, not even after Mother gave her a solemn order.

Finally, they all curled on the floor and slept as best they could in the fierce heat.

When the first rays of sunrise broke the darkness, Paul found Great Aunt Edna slumped in her chair only inches from the blank TV screen, her head hanging over the seatback, her skin purple, eyes bulging, her upper plate dropped onto her bloated tongue. As the rest of the family gathered, Paul expected them to become hysterical.

Instead Grandma clucked annoyance: "Of all times for this to happen." Mother retreated to the linen closet and came back with the family's worst sheet, the one with stains and frayed edges, to drape over the old woman.

Father pointed a finger at each of them, muttering numbers under his breath. He head snapped back when he realized that Martha stood among them. Then he counted again and pointed a finger at her. "Where's Grace?" he demanded.

"I lowered her out the window last night. I sent her for help."

Father slapped Martha so hard she tripped over Great Aunt Edna's rigid foot and jarred the false teeth onto the carpet.

"You fool!" Father roared. "We'll never see Grace again."

"I don't care," Grandma said. "I don't care about anything."

Mother threw a candlestick at the television screen and the room shook with the implosion. Father glared as if he would strike her too but instead opened his penknife and slashed great gashes across the back of the sofa, then pulled out handfuls of stuffing to rub into Grandma's hair. She yanked down the curtains and wrapped them around his neck. Martha, now in the kitchen, broke dishes, one at a time, sailing them out against the walls of the other rooms. Robert attacked the bathroom fixtures with the new wrench from his work tools, chipping porcelain across the tiles, shattering the lid of the commode, slivering the mirror.

Paul found himself in Mother and Father's room upending dresser drawers and ripping clothing from closet hangers. When he paused to look into their mirror, he saw that his mouth was wide open and recognized the sound that echoed from the walls as his own laughter. Then he stood at the window, about to smash the glass and toss Mother's jewelry box down to the garbage cans, when he heard the back doorbell. He stepped out into the hallway and saw that no one else noticed the long piercing ring. They were all grunting and heaving.

Father knocked Grandma to the floor and kneeled with a knee in her stomach as he fought to slip his knuckles under the knotted scarf she twisted against his windpipe. Martha had found Paul's secret magazines and was tearing them apart. Mother stood over the pages as they fluttered to the floor, shoving her fingers in her mouth but still screaming at what she saw. Robert rushed from behind Martha and hit her face until blood gushed from both nostrils.

The bell still screamed. Before Paul could reach the knob, the door swung open. There, centered on the fiber mat, sat a huge basket of fruit—luscious pears, gleaming red apples, oranges, bananas, plums, even mangos and pomegranates—all covered with bright yellow cellophane and topped with a satin bow. With great care, Paul opened the tiny envelope tucked against the straw and slid out the card. "From our family to yours," it said, "Welcome," signed "Mrs. A."

MISS WILCOX'S GHOST

The father stood at the window and watched the children, his among them, dash about the tombstones. They ran squealing down the overgrown paths, leapfrogging the smaller markers, ducking to hide behind the granite monuments, now and then stopping to puzzle at a weathered date, trying to trace out the shape of the numbers with a fingertip. He watched with the puzzlement he had moments before given the rooks that wheeled about the winter-barren trees, creatures of another order whose habits were strange and mysterious. He found it hard to believe that someday these children would end up like him.

He could not recall himself as a child; that is, he remembered details, events, but had years before lost the sense of how it felt to be a child. He wondered what these children thought about the untended graveyard that was their playground. Did they sense the fate of their village, the generations of Lays and Nashes, names of families still in the same houses, the ancestors and the ancestors of ancestors accumulating in stark rows? Did they feel the presence of death beneath their feet? Did it grasp at their shoes? Or could they run free of it? It numbed him just to look at the graves.

The day turned dark again. For an hour, the first in a week, the blue sky had broken clear beyond the trees, but now the clouds were back, merged into a mass of grey, like an iron lid stifling the village. The father sensed the clutch of gloom, as if he had just read his name on one of the stones. Even in his thick sweater he shivered, but remained at the window, watching.

His house bordered the church and the graveyard. It was known as the Old Rectory though no rector had lived there for the past twenty-five years. He was the fifth in a line of businessmen owners, people who did not stay long. Since the war the church population had dwindled, and the building, noted for its Norman door in the guidebooks, was visited more by antiquarians and brass-rubbers than by believers. No one cared for the property; weeds and nettles choked the yard. The door was never locked, but he had been inside only once himself. Everything around him was so old and overgrown. He felt he was dwelling in a place haunted by itself.

The children were the only ones who really used the church. They spent hours at a time inside, and the father had no idea of what they did. He tried to ask once; all they told him was that they never touched anything.

An old tithe barn sat across the graveyard, abandoned for a century, the wooden doors half-rotted, great holes in the roof where storms had blown the slates loose. It too was a favorite place of the children.

Now the children stopped their play, one by one rising from their hiding places behind the tombstones to stand fixed and let their gazes follow Rochelle's fingertip as it pointed up at the spire. An odd child, he thought, and felt a sympathy for her strangeness, as if he was closer to understanding her than any of the others. He heard only sounds of shouting, but could not make out the words. He wondered what she had seen.

———————————

"She's gone now," Rochelle said, her small voice clipped and rapid. "All your fussing frightened her away. But you did see her."

"There wasn't anything," Simon denied. He was one of two boys, he and John.

"I saw her," Mary said. "She was all in white."

"Yes, that's it!" Rochelle became excited. "She wears a white gown and a white bonnet."

"Why doesn't she dress like us?" Julie wanted to know. She put her thumb in her mouth and eyed the spire uneasily.

"Because she lived centuries ago, you silly girl," Diana said.

"Ah, Rochelle made it up about the white," Simon insisted. John nodded beside him.

"No," Diana said. "I've heard my parents talk about her. She's been a legend in the village forever so long. They say she always fancied white when she was alive."

"My granddad saw her once when he was a boy," Margaret added.

I think she's quite beautiful," Rochelle said.

"How can she be?" John taunted. "She was an old lady."

"But she was young and beautiful once. She's beautiful to me."

"You're a queer girl," Simon said.

"That's because ghosts like me." Rochelle turned her back and walked away from them. She wore a party dress and looked quite fragile.

Margaret invented a new game. "There she is! Behind that bush. Let's catch her." And the others, knowing that Margaret had seen nothing, ran off after the ghost.

Later, tired and breathless with giggling, they tumbled into a patch of weeds behind the newest of the grave mounds. Sitting cross-legged or sprawled on their stomachs, they wrapped their scarves higher around their necks and pulled on their mittens. Simon plucked a dry stalk and sucked it between his teeth. John watched him closely and did the same thing.

"We'll never catch her," Margaret said.

"People can't catch ghosts," Mary told her.

Julie pointed at the grave mound. "Who's buried there?"

Simon flipped a twig end over end at the heap of pale brown dirt. "Her? She's old Mrs. Lunt from one of the farms. She was well into her eighties and hadn't been out of the house in years. I never saw her alive."

"Is she the ghost?" Julie asked.

The others all laughed. "Mrs. Lunt?" They laughed for quite a while, as if Julie could not have said anything funnier. When they quieted, Diana told her, "Miss Wilcox is the ghost."

"But when did she die?" Julie spoke uncertainly. She was new to the village and shy, embarrassed by the loss of her front baby teeth.

She died the same year as King Charles the Second," Margaret said.

"But why is she a ghost?"

Diana knew the story. "Miss Wilcox was the most beautiful young lady for miles around, in the whole county. She was engaged to a handsome officer. He rode off one morning and told her he would be home in time for supper. But he never came back, and no one ever heard of him. For five years Miss Wilcox smiled and looked beautiful as if nothing had happened. Then one morning she woke up screaming that she had lost something. She rushed around looking all over the house and in the garden. She wouldn't tell anyone what it was she had lost. From that morning on she spent the rest of her life looking about the village ten hours a day, even when she became a very old ugly lady. And they say her ghost has come out every night since she died to keep on looking."

"But how do they know she's a ghost?" Julie asked.

"Because people have seen her," Mary said.

Simon scoffed. "Loonies have seen her."

"William Runting and Adam Simpson saw her."

"They say! Let me tell you what really happened. Last spring when the trees were in blossom, they came here after school to play and saw something white moving up in the top of that tree right over there by the church door. They rushed straight back to school screaming for the headmaster. He hopped on his bicycle and they ran in the road after him. Do you know what he found?"

"No. What'?"

"A flock of white birds in the treetop. They all flew away, and there went your ghost."

"And then there's Alfred Bolling the carpenter." John started to tell that story, but Simon interrupted.

"Last Whitsun eve Alfred Bolling was walking across the fields from Barrington. He'd spent most of the night at the Marlborough Arms and took a notion to top it off with a few at the Hand and Shears. It was quite foggy that night, and right in the middle of the field he saw a large grey shape not ten yards ahead of him. He was too scared to run, so he tiptoed not to give himself away. But the shape moved along right with him. Alfred screamed for mercy. He bolted, but couldn't see where he was going in the fog and ended up rushing about in circles. Finally, he ran right into the grey shape."

"Ugggh!" Julie said.

"It was only a mule," Simon laughed. "A dumb mule."

"But what about Mrs. Leigh," Mary said. "She wasn't drunk. She's never been drunk in her life."

"What happened?"

"One night two or three years ago she heard the organ being played in the church. When she looked out her window, the church was dark. She thought it was one of us children doing what we weren't supposed to. So she put on her coat and walked across the road straight up to the church door. The closer she got, the louder the music was. But when she threw open the door to scold, the music suddenly stopped and there wasn't anyone at the keyboard."

"Wind," Simon said.

"Wind indeed!"

"Rochelle saw her," Julie said.

"Rochelle sees ghosts all the time," John mocked, "if you believe what she tells you. Rochelle is bonkers."

Simon had an idea. "Let's make Rochelle admit that she just pretends to see ghosts. Let's put her to the test."

"What if she's telling the truth?" Mary asked

"Rochelle is the biggest liar in the village."

"You won't hurt her," Margaret said. "I won't play if you hurt her."

"It's just a game," Simon answered.

Rochelle was lying flat in the weeds behind the row of Nash tombstones. When she saw the others heading for her, she ran out toward the gate to the road. Simon caught her. He was surprised how light she was, how easy to pick up and carry. She tried to slap his face, but he barely felt her hands as he wondered where to take her. He decided on the old tithe barn.

———————

The father waited at the window, hoping the children would reappear. They had talked for a long time, and he could not imagine what they were saying to one another. Then they got up to prowl about the tombstones looking for something. Finally, they ran around to the other side of the church, out of his range of vision.

It struck him that he had not seen Rochelle with them, and he began to ponder that strange girl. Though older than most of the others, she was the smallest of the group, light as a wisp, quite fragile, with hair so fine it was almost transparent, always wearing starched dresses that accentuated her spindly legs. Some days the others, especially Simon, teased her cruelly, perhaps because her feelings were so easily hurt and she was so quick to cry.

She claimed to see ghosts they told him. Perhaps she did. With her tight serious mouth and her tales of old gossip, she wasn't like a child. Perhaps she was already disenchanted with childhood, ghost obsessed, longing to become a ghost herself, already aware she would not come to much as a human being.

The father sensed that he was close to comprehending her. But when he closed his eyes to make a last mental grasp, his thoughts scattered like a flock of vanishing birds. Tempted to give up watching and sit down, he still waited for the children to return because he had nothing else to do.

———————

Inside, the tithe barn was a litter of trash, smashed slates, splintered wood, old rusted tools, loose heaps of straw, piles of yellow newspapers. Small birds flapped in and out of the holes in the roof. John caught a baby mouse in his cap, but Simon made him let it go. He stood Rochelle against a hand-hewn upright beam in the center of the barn. The others formed a circle around her. Her pale blue eyes were wide with defiance, staring hard at each one in turn, but her lips quivered, and they all knew she was struggling not to cry. "What do you want of me?" she said.

"We don't want you around," John said. "You're not like us."

"I'm better than you."

Simon stung her bare legs with a twig.

"You promised you wouldn't hurt her," Margaret said.

"That didn't hurt, did it, Rochelle?"

She would not answer.

"Do you know why we don't like you'?"

"You're jealous."

Simon forced a laugh. "Because you lie. You lie about everything. You lie about talking to ghosts."

"I do talk to ghosts."

He swatted her legs harder. "Talk now. Talk to Miss Wilcox."

"She won't talk with you around. She told me she hates you."

"Miss Wilcox," John whined in falsetto. "Miss Wilcox, where are you now? Are you really Rochelle's mother? Is Rochelle a ghost too?"

"I don't like this," Mary said.

"Why not?"

"It isn't nice to make fun of people."

"There she is!" Rochelle called, and pointed to a dark corner.

Margaret screamed, "Ohhhh," and the five of them stood frozen until Simon took a few steps toward the darkness. "I don't see a thing."

"She's gone," Diana said.

"Miss Wilcox'?"

"No, Rochelle."

"See," Simon cried, "she is a liar! A sneak and a cheat."

They ran back out into the graveyard to catch her. The sun was beginning to set behind the clouds at the horizon and the tombstones lay deep in shadows. They looked quietly and carefully, stalking all the hiding places.

"Maybe she went home," Margaret said.

"No. We would have seen her in the road."

Then Mary noticed that the door to the church was open slightly. Simon put a finger to his lips to silence them and led them into the church on tiptoe. They squatted behind the pews at the back, just beside the large stone font.

A heavy darkness hung over the damp building, except for the light that filtered through the stained glass window. Directly in its rays, Rochelle kneeled on the carpet in front of the altar in an attitude of private prayer. But she was not speaking to God.

"They're wicked children, Miss Wilcox. They're quite mean to me. They won't believe in you. But I know what you can do. When they're asleep in their beds at night and their houses are still, you go to them. Haunt their lives. Make them ugly and miserable. Make them empty."

Simon trembled with anger; he wanted to rush forward and slap her face. But they were inside the church. When Margaret, Mary, Diana, Julie, and John slipped back out through the door into the grey twilight, he followed them.

Mary sobbed frantically beside a tombstone. "Oh, I'm so scared."

Margaret tried to soothe her with a stroking embrace.

"Don't believe her," Simon insisted. "If anybody is going to be haunted, it will be Rochelle. "

"I know what we can do," John said. "Let's ask a grownup."

The father, whose hands now felt the chill of evening seeping through the window frame, saw the children appear from the side of the church as shadows. When he noticed the determination in their walks, he knew they would be coming straight to him. He stopped them in the doorway. "Wipe your shoes on the mat." He had no idea what they wanted, but hoped he could evade them.

They all spoke at once.

"Are there such things as ghosts?"

"Does Miss Wilcox have a ghost?"

"Is Rochelle a ghost?"

"Can she make Miss Wilcox haunt us?"

His first impulse was to smile, but he could not. Their young faces were both comic and touching in their gravity. Excited to hear his words, they expected a serious answer from him. His answer would be very important to them. He felt the oppression of an unwanted burden, and he wasn't sure how much to tell them.

"What do you think?" he asked.

"Ghosts are nonsense," Simon said.

"I believe," Mary whispered, her eyes still wet with tears.

The father looked out the window for several moments at the half moon beyond the church spire. He turned back to the children. "Most people are completely wrong about ghosts. Ghosts are not spirits of the past, but rather of the future. They are what we are going to become. That is what really frightens us."

"Then," John said, "is Miss Wilcox really Rochelle's ghost? A ghost who spends all her time looking for something she's lost?"

"Every ghost looks for something it's lost. That's what ghosts are all about. Ghosts don't haunt other people. They haunt themselves.

"What is your ghost, Daddy?" one of the children who was his own asked him. The father met his unmoving reflection in the window glass. "I am," he said.

CALL HER

A fierce March wind stung his face, so frigid it burned. From the observation platform, Wallace stared out at snow-laden peaks, Alpine crests layered back to the horizon, their whiteness blinding under an azure sky. Though he stood far from the platform's edge, gloved hands locked on a metal railing, his mind swirled with a fear of plunging into a glacial crevasse. He had to turn away. Behind him, within the glass walls of the revolving restaurant, diners sat warm at their tables, garish ski jackets draped over chair backs, mouths moving in a Babel of languages, heads thrown back in laughter. But he couldn't hear a word, only the howl that lashed his flesh with invisible particles. He winced and gritted teeth, as if pain were the price of such awful beauty.

Wallace pulled back the band of his sleeve to check his watch—two p.m.—and wondered what time it was back home. Eight p.m. or eight a.m.? Time zones bewildered him. He was never sure which direction he had traveled, reverse or ahead. His confusion always annoyed Lucille. He wanted to call her now, from a mountain top, but worried that it was the middle of the night for her. He might wake Sally's baby too. How could you know when a newborn was sleeping? Lucille would be furious. Why was Lucille there and he here, experiencing this alone? He wanted to roar his frustration into the icy whorl.

Wallace realized a young man was grinning at him from out at the edge of the concrete terrace, under a spinning wind vane. Had he spoken aloud? Had the young man heard his thoughts? The man stood hatless, jacket open, leaning forward with arms spread as if welcoming the blasts that swirled his thick red hair. He nodded at Wallace and began to walk toward him, a hand outstretched in greeting.

Wallace let the bare hand grasp his glove, welcoming the human contact. The young man had a pointed face, tanned and blue-eyed, a narrow red beard outlining his jaw.

"I'm Chet," he said. "I couldn't help noticing we're the only two people on this mountain without skis."

"I've never skied in my life," Wallace said after he introduced himself, shouting over the rush of the wind.

"I do whenever I get the chance. But all this"—Chet pointed toward the figures gliding down the mountainside—"is a surprise. I didn't expect to be here today."

"Where were you supposed to be?"

"Nowhere. I mean wherever I want to go. So I ended up in this spectacular place. There's so much in the world to surprise us. So many possibilities."

"It's my tenth trip to Europe," Wallace told him, "but I've never seen anything like this."

"Why's that?"

Wallace turned his back to the mountains. "It's always been for business. Meetings. Nothing but conference rooms and hotels."

Chet touched his shoulder. "Is this business? Now? Up here? Are we having a meeting?"

I'm not alone any more, Wallace thought, but decided not to say it aloud.

———————————

Chet edged him into a doorway out of the freezing blasts. Wallace began shivering, the chill like needles in his joints, an uncontrollable tremor running through his body. He clasped the metal doorframe with both hands and held tight.

"That happens sometimes," Chet said. "Delayed reaction. A thing's already over, and then you feel the effects."

When Wallace stopped trembling, he felt damp with sweat, wiped his face with the sleeve of his parka. "This is supposed to be a vacation. Planned for six months. I'd make my contacts in Zurich, and then my wife would fly over for a week of travel."

Chet glanced toward the dining room. "Is she inside?"

Wallace shook his head. "Hardly. Her daughter's baby came early. She's back home. Gaga at being a grandmother."

"And you a grandfather?"

"Not quite. It's my stepdaughter. From her first marriage."

"And you can't be with them."

"Work doesn't stop because somebody has a baby."

"So your wife chose the baby over the scenery."

"I timed this trip to happen weeks before the due date."

"You're really pissed about that kid." Chet shook his head.

"I shouldn't be. It wasn't deliberate. It's nobody's fault."

"But it took you by surprise."

"Lucille should be here."

Chet unzipped his jacket and pulled out a thin mobile phone with a wide screen. "This takes great pictures. You could call Lucille right now and show her the view. All that she's missing."

"I have a cell phone," Wallace told him.

"Not like this one. It has amazing features. And it's vital in my work."

"Which is?"

"Bringing people together. Making connections. That's what I do." Chet leaned forward and pressed the phone into Wallace's gloved palm. "Take it. I've got several with me. You can do so much with it. Play with the options."

Wallace hesitated, but Chet brought a hand over his and closed the fingers with a firm pressure.

————————

Chet invited Wallace to walk in the snow. When they descended the stairway to the base of the building, they found no paths, just a narrow clearing where skiers prepared for the downhill run. One by one the skiers pushed themselves off, gathered speed to a rise fifty yards off, and then disappeared behind a white crest.

"See what you're missing?" Chet said.

"I'd end up in a body cast. Why do they do it?"

"Risk gives some people great pleasure."

"Couldn't you rent skis?"

"No need. I've met you."

They waited for the cable car down to Mürren. In the middle of the afternoon, on the boarding platform, they were the only ones going in that direction, waiting for the arriving skiers to shuffle out of the gondola with their boot-stiff gaits. Inside the car Chet leaned close to the plastic window, grinning down at the world below, and Wallace followed his eyes, not sure what he was seeing.

Once at the base, they walked the narrow snow-packed streets through the town to the train station, and there Chet suggested they continue on foot to the funicular, his face suddenly bright, as if the idea had just struck him. They could look out at the mountains that towered across the valley. It would take an hour, but Wallace had no other plans, and he was really glad for the company, someone to talk to. Chet walked quickly, and Wallace was limping by the time they reached the platform for the funicular. Down in Lauterbrunnen, they boarded the waiting train back to Interlaken, sitting side by side, Chet going on about his phones and Wallace straining to keep his eyes open, unable to follow the explanations.

"Which hotel are you in?" Chet asked.

"The Bernerhof. This isn't on the expense account."

"I'm in the Victoria."

Wallace raised eyebrows. "Nice."

"I'm indulging myself," Chet told him. "What do you say I pick you up for dinner about, say, seven-thirty? My treat. Like you say, it's no fun eating alone."

"I need a nap."

"Don't forget to call Lucille," Chet said, when he turned off on the path to the canopied entrance of the Victoria.

"What time is it there?" Wallace looked at his watch, then shook his head.

"Beats me." Chet shrugged.

Wallace didn't have much appetite, but Chet ordered a plate heaped with sausage and rösti and a large beer stein. It made Wallace queasy to watch him eat, the way the man bent close to the plate and loaded his mouth with one forkful after another. Then he thought he wasn't being fair. The man was just enjoying the food. Maybe his head was swimming from altitude sickness. He had no idea what that would be like, but something was making him feel strange.

"I'm waiting for a woman." Chet sat back in his chair and took a long swig from the stein, wiping foam with the back of his hand.

"What woman?"

"Someone I met in London. Nicole. Actually I knew her— slightly. She does the same thing I do. She says she'll join me here, in Interlaken. And tomorrow's supposed to be the day. That is, she may show up. She said she would, but you never can tell with women."

"Don't you have anybody back home?"

"Nicht. No wife, no stepdaughter, no grandchild. It gives me latitude."

"Nothing in the way of your pleasure."

Chet lifted his stein in a toast. "Here's to indulgence."

———————————

The room phone rang just as Wallace was stepping out of the shower, wrapping himself in a thick white towel. The clock on the night table read 9 a.m. He picked up the receiver about to say "Lucille," but heard his name pronounced in foreign syllables. "This is reception," the woman said. "There are people here calling for you."

"For me? Who?"

He heard a sharp thud, as if someone dropped the phone, then a scraping. "Wallace. It's me, Chet. Come on down."

In the elevator, Wallace wondered what he could want. Wasn't the woman from London supposed to be arriving? Maybe she changed her mind, and they could spend the day together.

When he stepped out into the lobby, he saw Chet beside the postcard rack, a young woman at his side, the two of them in identical red parkas.

"Meet Nicole," Chet said, gesturing from her to Wallace and back again. "I told you all about her."

Despite the pale face and thin lips, the close-cropped auburn hair that looked hacked by a dull scissors, Wallace found himself drawn to her. Large plastic earrings dangled from her lobes, the same color as her dark eyes. Her parka spread open as she arched back with her hands in the hip pockets of her jeans, her small breasts taut in a black turtleneck. For an instant, Wallace wished Chet wasn't there, that she had come for him.

When he took her extended hand, it was cold. "And Chet's told me about your grandchild. Congratulations." Her voice was high, staccato, the accent not British, but nothing he could place.

"It's my stepdaughter's."

"Still, there's cause for celebration." She broke the word into syllables, lingering over each.

Chet wrapped his arm about Nicole and Wallace's shoulders, pulled them together. "That's why we're here. To help you celebrate."

"There's no need. You've just arrived." Wallace looked at Nicole for a reaction. "I'm sure you and Chet have things you'd rather do together."

"Nonsense." She pressed his hand. "We'll make a day of it."

"Get your coat," Chet said. "I've got plans."

Wallace took the stairs, not waiting for the elevator. He wouldn't have to be by himself.

On the street outside the hotel, a pale blue Opel sat idling at the curb, the driver's door wide open, a deep rusted gash in the rear quarter panel. "Hop in," Chet said.

"Where did this come from?" Wallace peered inside and saw empty shopping bags strewn on the back seat, rags on the floor.

"I rented it."

"A car like this?"

"Chet enjoys the unusual." Nicole grinned, thick gums surrounding cramped teeth. "He's a very ingenious person."

At Chet's signal, Wallace sat in the front, leaning forward so that Nicole could climb in back. But she squeezed in beside him despite the narrow bucket seats, her thigh tight against his, forcing his knee against the shift lever.

"Is this legal?" he asked.

She shrugged. "How should I know? I'm a foreigner."

They drove past the train station at Interlaken Ost where a crowd gathered on the platform, carrying skis zipped into cloth cases, old people, children. The skiers walked with a hunched, stiff-kneed tilt, plastic boot heels wobbling against the concrete. Despite their ungainliness, Wallace had a sensation that he was the odd one, a stranger groping for balance.

"Where are we going?" he asked

"Up into the mountains," Chet told him.

"Consider us your guides." Nicole massaged the back of his neck. He stopped himself from touching her leg.

"Did you call Lucille?" Chet asked him.

"Not yet. I'm waiting for the right time."

Nicole closed a hand on his arm. "I thought you missed your wife."

"He's furious with her," Chet said, "for choosing her daughter over him."

"Hey, it's not like that. She has an obligation."

"Ring her up," Nicole urged. "Later today. We won't let you forget."

Chet drove up a narrow road barely the width of a single car, the pavement clear but snow piled high on both sides, above the roof. Wallace felt the strain of the climb, the engine whining in second gear. Nicole leaned forward, urging sounds in her throat, her nose almost touching the windshield.

"Do you know where we are?" Wallace asked Chet.

"Absolutely."

"He imprints maps," Nicole added.

The road widened and a parking area opened on their left. Chet wrenched the steering wheel as on a sudden urge, the back wheels churning a cloud of snow. He switched off the engine and swung open the door. When Wallace got out, he stretched and flexed his knees, unsteady in the snow, missing the contact with Nicole.

Dozens of skis were stacked beside a pylon, directly ahead a steady stream of skiers dropping off the T-bars and disappearing downhill. Wallace followed Chet and Nicole as they took seats on a wooden platform across from a sprawling hotel painted a drab green. Chet ordered mugs of coffee that drifted steam into the chill air. But the day was bright. All around them people sprawled on chairs with heads back and faces turned up toward the sun.

Chet took a pair of binoculars from his backpack and peered down into the valley, constantly adjusting the focus. Wallace wondered what he was trying to see.

"How many stepchildren do you have?" Nicole asked him.

"Three. Sally and two sons. None of them live close. So we don't see them often. They were all gone when Lucille and I married."

"How sad for her."

"She's on the phone with them all the time. Three or four times a week."

"So you never got a chance to really know them yourself."

"They're adults. The same age as you and Chet."

"My mum rarely calls."

"Everybody's different." Chet did not take the lenses from his eyes.

"Any children of your own?" Nicole said.

"Two. A boy and a girl. But they don't have much interest in hearing from me."

"Why's that?

"I left their mother for Lucille."

"How romantic!" Nicole threw her head back.

"All I remember now are lawyers and people screaming at one another."

"But it was worth it. You have the woman you truly love." Nicole covered his gloved hand with hers. "That's what really matters in life, doesn't it?" She was looking at Chet with narrowed eyes.

Chet stood abruptly, climbed onto a chair, and leaned forward. "Wow! What a flip. Tangled skis. Head in a snowbank. Broken bones. Or torn ligaments for certain. Anybody else want to see?" Nicole snatched the binoculars from him.

––––––––––––

Chet headed toward the hotel. "Be back in a while."

Nicole popped open her parka and squinted up at the sun's rays. "Isn't it wonderful here?"

"Why do you and Chet match?" Wallace asked.

She gave him a puzzled look.

"Your jackets."

"Oh those. Absolute coincidence. We laughed and laughed when we saw each other."

"How did you get here so early today? Last night he wasn't even sure that you would come."

Nicole smiled, baring her gums. "Oh, I've been here all along."

"I don't understand."

"Chet always likes to play tricks on me," she said. "And now I'm getting back. Making him wonder about me."

"He said you didn't know each other very well."

"You have to take Chet with a grain of salt. What else did he tell you about us?"

"That you both do the same thing."

"He said that, did he?" Nicole gave an abrupt laugh.

"What do you do?"

"He wasn't far off. I like to send messages too."

––––––––––––

When Chet came back, he pointed his mobile phone at Wallace, aiming to take a photo. "Click," he said and showed the screen to the others. Without realizing it, Wallace had brought a hand over his face. Only his startled eyes were visible.

Nicole got up as soon as Chet sat down. "Which way are the

loos?" He pointed.

"What's going on with you two?" Wallace said when she walked away, more annoyed than puzzled.

"Nothing. Why? What did she tell you?"

"That you play tricks on one another."

"I think you're the one she's playing a trick on. I hardly know the woman."

"Are you lovers?"

Chet laughed. He pointed at Wallace and laughed louder, tears in his eyes. He put his face down in his arms on the tabletop and his body quivered.

They ate lunch in the hotel, seated in a shadowed corner of a narrow dining room with dark brown walls, far from the bright windows. Wallace found the food dull and heavy, thick grease on the plate, but Chet and Nicole both scooped up large forkfuls and left nothing. "Altitude makes me starved," Chet said. Nicole nodded. "There's nothing wrong with my appetites." She hissed the "s" and arranged the empty beer bottles on a place mat, each one placed carefully, as if she had a pattern in mind.

"Excuse me." Chet pushed back his chair and walked out to the lobby. Wallace could see him talking to the man behind the desk, half hidden by the edge of the doorway.

"What damn game are you two playing?" Wallace locked on to Nicole's eyes. "You tell me one thing and he tells me another."

"It's not a game. Whatever we do is serious."

"Are you or aren't you lovers?"

"That depends how you define it. Let's just say that we need each other."

"For what?"

"To be who we are."

It was Chet's idea that they walk in the snow. Wallace had been hesitant to endure more cold but Nicole insisted, linking her arm in his and almost pulling him out the door. Once on the trail she dropped his arm and stepped away. After a half hour, he looked back to see the hotel had disappeared behind a peak of jagged grey rock, bare of snow. Chet and Nicole pulled up their parka hoods, fixed straps under their chins. Walking behind them, Wallace wished he had remembered to take a hat, but they had rushed him out of the hotel. His ears felt like ice, brittle.

Far down in the valley he could see the skiers, tiny shapes arcing across the whiteness. Out here the world seemed vaster than he had ever imagined. For a second, he stood rooted on the path and shuddered with a sensation of awful aloneness.

Nicole began to run after Chet, chasing him. He stopped abruptly, reached both arms into a drift and tossed a large scoop at her. She grabbed at snow with gloved hands, quickly squeezing it into icy clumps and throwing them at him, one after another. Chet lunged to topple her backwards, then straddled her waist and rubbed fistfuls of snow into her face. Wallace expected screams, but Nicole didn't make a sound, didn't struggle for freedom.

On an impulse, he moved to help her. "Hey!" he called, about to seize Chet by the shoulders. But before he could reach out, the two of them turned on him, Chet locking his arms behind his back, Nicole heaving hard-packed chunks at him.

It was a child's game, but no one was laughing. Then Chet said, "Do you give up?"

Wallace gave a fierce nod. "Yes. Of course." And he was released.

"We won!" Nicole cried. She toppled backwards and swung out her arms and legs to form a snow angel.

———————

For dinner they sat almost at the same table where they had eaten lunch, just one over. All the others were filled, everyone else speaking Swiss Deutsch and hoisting beer steins. Fireplace logs crackled and exploded sparks. Chet and Nicole ordered raclette, wide plates with tiny onions swimming in melted cheese. They dipped bread chunks and washed it down with long gulps. Wallace wanted only a sandwich.

"Time to get in touch," Chet said. He turned to Wallace with a dark expression. "Where's the phone I gave you."

"In my hotel room. You rushed me out."

Wallace expected Chet to be angry, but he lifted his sweater and pulled out his own phone. With a fingertip, he touched the screen and a keypad appeared. Then he reached the phone toward Wallace. "Want to call anyone?"

"Or you can use mine." Nicole took an identical phone from her canvas bag and placed it in Wallace's hand.

He rubbed his fingertips over the pattern of keys, pressed one by mistake and pulled back at the sudden beep. "Could you actually make calls from a place like this? So remote."

Chet nodded. "There no such thing as remote any more. Lucille is only a few tones away."

"Call her," Nicole urged.

"No. Not now." Wallace shook his head. "Not from here."

She closed both her hands over the phone in his, pressed an edge into his palm. "I don't think you truly love Lucille. You never want to talk to her, and we're making it so easy."

"How could I explain all this? Where I am." He laid the phone on the table.

"Tell her you're with us," Chet said.

─────────────

After the dishes were cleared and the waitress poured coffee, Chet took out a cigar, bit off the end, and offered it to Wallace. Wallace held up a hand. "I don't . . ." Nicole grabbed it, and Chet produced another, then lit hers and his, the two of them exhaling thick, pungent smoke toward the center of the table. Wallace couldn't see their faces behind the clouds.

The smell was making him sick to his stomach. He stood up. "Why don't we head back to Interlaken? Before it gets dark."

"Sit down," Chet reached out to grip Wallace's arm, pulling him back into the chair.

Nicole touched his wrist. "We're not going back tonight. That's another surprise."

"I don't understand."

"Chet booked us a room."

Wallace looked to the door with an impulse to walk out on them. "Why didn't you consult me?"

"Then it wouldn't be a surprise."

"Take me back," he insisted.

"In the morning," Chet said. "It wouldn't be safe with me now. I've had too much to drink."

If the lobby had chairs, Wallace would have sat there all night. But the space was cramped and barren, just a narrow counter and a rack of keys. A few people gathered around the bar at the far end of the entrance area. He didn't want a drink or conversation. How could he tell people that he didn't know where he was, that two strangers had trapped him in this place?

His coat under his arm, he climbed the steep stairway, slowly, one at a time, aching in his thighs. He paused at the landing to look down a dim hallway, then took the next flight and found the room number Chet had given him. He closed his hand on the doorknob and tapped, more loudly when no one responded. Finally, he pushed the door back and saw a double bed and a cot, brown wool blankets pulled tight across both.

In the dim light of a single lamp, Chet sat cross-legged on a wood rail chair, Nicole on the floor, pressed into a corner next to a dark wardrobe. Each spoke into one of the tiny phones.

"Hello, Nicole. Where are you?"

"Hi, Chet. I'm in a hotel in the Alps. What about you?"

"A hotel in the Alps too."

"Life's just one big coincidence."

"Isn't it though?"

They pretended to ignore Wallace's entrance, but he knew they were performing for him.

"What can you tell me about our friend Wallace?" Chet said.

"He's not a happy man."

"And why is that?"

"Bad marriage to the wrong woman. That makes two in a row. He never learns."

"Someone should teach him a lesson."

"Shouldn't someone just."

"You're not funny." Wallace resisted the urge to slap the phones away from their faces. "You don't know anything about my marriage. About my life."

"You don't call her, Wallace." Nicole let out an exasperated sigh.

"It's so easy to talk." Chet cupped his hands and offered the phone. Wallace brushed it aside.

———————————

Chet told them he was going down for a drink. Wallace expected Nicole to follow, but she pulled her legs close to her shoulders and rested her chin on her knees.

"Why didn't he get two rooms?" Wallace asked her when the door closed.

"I don't think you really want another room."

"Of course, I do. Why should I be here with you and Chet?"

Nicole unfolded herself and stood up, smoothing the turtleneck against her stomach. "The double bed is for us, you know."

"What!" He felt himself sinking, legs weak, and gripped the wardrobe handle. "I can't. I don't want to."

"We know how you've been staring at me." She reached down and pulled the turtleneck loose from her belt.

Scarred. The thought startled Wallace: if her body hadn't been covered by a layer of clothing, he would see scars, the marks of deep wounds.

Wallace turned away, faced the crude painting of a mountain peak on the wall in front of him, the icy crevices just thick shadowed globs. He refused to look at her. She reached around him, one hand around his waist, the other on his throat. Even through his sweater and thick

41

corduroy trousers he could feel the heat of her flesh. The room was terribly cold, no warmth from the pipes. He wondered why she wasn't freezing.

"No!" he shouted, about to throw her off. Just then Chet swung the door open, banged it against the wall, and slammed it shut. His red hair swirled in a wild tangle, ice crystals glistening in his beard. Wallace expected the man to hit him, to curse him and crush a fist into his face. Instead, a phone's camera flash dazzled his eyes.

Chet was laughing. "You'll never guess what I did."

"What?" The way Nicole said it, she already knew.

"I called Lucille, sent her this picture the instant I took it."

"You're lying!" Wallace wouldn't look. He knocked the phone from Chet's hand. "You don't know her daughter's name, her number."

"It's in your wallet." Chet pulled the folded leather from a pocket and tossed it at Wallace.

Nicole pressed against his back and held him tighter, her body writhing against him as if in pain.

"I woke the baby," Chet said. "I told her about Nicole. Lucille's very angry. She doesn't want you back."

Nicole's whisper rasped against his ear. "She doesn't care if you rot here."

"Goddamn you! Damn you both!" Wallace swung out, his arm crashing the lamp to the floor. The bulb exploded and the darkness was total. In the silence he heard only his heartbeat and felt the force of their presences just inches away.

Wallace bolted, seeing nothing, slapping at the walls, groping until he found the door and tumbled into the hallway, down the stairs, shoes clattering the worn wood, then out into the night. The intense cold shocked him. Shudders racked his body like an electric current. He had left his coat behind, heaped on the floor. He had never been so cold, so frozen.

Gazing at the dark shapes of the mountains, he could not stop his shaking, the wind lashing his face. Rows of T-bar pylons stood outlined in the moonlight, and beyond, miles away, pinpricks of light dotted a village in the valley. Far above him a million tiny stars shone bright in a frigid sky.

When he turned, Wallace saw hotel windows glowing behind drawn curtains. Were Chet and Nicole peeking around the edges of the cloth, watching him? In the black of the room, terrified, he had been sure they would kill him. Now he imagined them laughing, clinging to one another with howls of satisfaction.

He walked back to the building, hungry for warmth, with no idea how he would find his way home, what he would discover when he arrived.

IN THE OLD VILLAGE

As dawn cast a dim light over the room, Karlik found himself sitting on a wooden bench, one of several rows in a small wooden building of bare beams and raw lathing. He was wearing a grey suit of a heavy coarse fabric, the trouser creases like ridges beneath his damp palms. The material gave off a sweet, oily odor. Sunrays filtered in through a single small window of ancient panes high in one wall. When Karlik looked around him, he saw the room was filled with people from his old village, the men also in dark suits, posed as he was with hands on their knees, leaning forward, but looking down at the broad splintered floor boards, none meeting his eyes. The women stared straight ahead, expressionless, some twisting beaded necklaces at their throats. But he had left this village many years before and had no memory of the trip back. His life was in the city.

Before Karlik could speak, ask what was happening, he heard someone tugging at the doors on one side of the building, a creaking at the hinges. He expected people to get up to help from inside, push their shoulders against the stubborn wood. But no one moved. He found his body rocking back and forth, just slightly, mimicking the movement of the doors. When they broke open with a loud cracking, as if the wood had splintered, he gasped and quickly covered his mouth. None of the others made a sound.

Four old men stood in the entranceway, peering inside, measuring space. Karlik blinked and remembered who they were, how much they had aged, shrunken, the flesh of their faces collapsed, their suits hanging on thin bones. After a moment they nodded at each other and moved back out of sight, only to reappear with a large wooden crate hoisted on their shoulders. They stepped through the doorway, clenching their jaws, staggering under the weight. Why wasn't anyone helping, Karlik wondered, the younger ones, the men like himself. He wanted to rise and go to them but could not move.

Shuffling across the floor, barely lifting their feet, they took a very long time to reach the center of the room and finally kneel to set the crate on two of the benches that had been moved forward, out of place. Three of the old men stepped backwards until they stood pressed against the lathing of the front wall. But the fourth went back outside and, in a moment, returned with a wooden toolbox. He picked out a mallet and a notched iron lever and held them up to the sunlight, as if assuring that he had chosen correctly.

The old man positioned the lever under the crate top and swung the mallet. The iron rang against the metal of a nail. He swung again and pried upward, swinging and prying, moving the lever around the edge of the crate, raising the top bit by bit. Karlik saw that he was the only one in the room watching the man's progress, flinching at each swing of the mallet. Yet he was mesmerized, barely daring to breathe.

When the top was loosened, the other three old men stepped forward to help lift it, and Karlik realized the wooden box was not a crate at all, but a coffin, a body inside, face in shadow, only the flesh of folded hands visible. It must be a funeral. He was back in his village for a funeral.

The building darkened, the sunlight suddenly gone. Karlik glanced up toward the window, expecting to see heavy clouds. But it was the branches of a huge tree swaying in a fierce wind, blocking the light, and seconds later letting it stream past. Darkness and brilliance alternated within the room, so rapidly Karlik felt dizzy, gritting his teeth and swallowing again and again to hold back the nausea.

In one of the flashes, when the room glowed, he thought the sides of the coffin were quivering, the ends sliding backwards. Then a long darkness, and he was not sure. But at the next moment of light, the ends dropped to the floor, the clatter resonating from the rafters. Both sides teetered and the darkness returned. Karlik heard their fall, first one and then the other.

Now he could see the body flat and rigid on the benches, dressed in a grey suit very much like the one he was wearing, the exposed skin of the hands and face dark and leathery. He wanted to speak, to tell the old men to repair the coffin, that what was happening was an outrage. But before he could open his mouth, the body began to twitch, first the arms rising with stiff, halting movements, then the trunk. The corpse was lifting itself, and the others just waited as if nothing were happening.

Darkness returned, but only for a second, and now the light penetrated, dazzling in its intensity. The corpse turned its face to Karlik, straightened an arm and pointed directly at him, empty eyes fixed on his. It was his father, a man who had been buried long before this day. A message had reached him in the city years ago: "Your father is dead." Karlik remembered it. He was sure it had happened.

"You!" Karlik heard the word roared, the sound like a thunder that shook the room. He rose and plunged forward, tumbling people from the bench in front of him. At last he could speak. "Stop this!" he cried out to the old men. "Stop this now!" The others began to moan, everyone in the room, steady, in unison, louder and louder. All light disappeared. Darkness was total, and hands fell upon him.

THE PEACOCK IN THE GARDEN

Mr. Buckler didn't call the peacock anything. A peacock wasn't a creature you could name, any more than you could name a sunset. Peacocks were to watch and wonder at. All his life, from his first rapt stares as a small boy at a cramped city zoo, their splendor had fascinated him. And now that he had moved to a village cottage bought with his disability settlement, a peacock lived in his garden.

His property was bleak with its cottage of dark stone, its dirt path, its yard of dull weeds, surrounded by brown fields under a slate sky. But suddenly, in the midst of this drabness the peacock would spread his dazzling brilliance. Mr. Buckler lingered for hours at his window to await its flourishing.

———————

He had selected this village from a map because its name suggested a great openness far from the city where he had spent his life. The first sight of his garden had brought him near to weeping. But he couldn't make things grow. Shrubbery never took root; flowers never blossomed. But he craved color, and so found his peacock, amazed that the crumpled bills he wadded into a stranger's fist could purchase such splendor.

———————

Every morning Mr. Buckler paced stiffly from edge to edge of his property. The doctors had told him the walking was a necessary exercise for a man with a spinal fusion. He wished the peacock would follow in his path, but the bird strutted aloof and apart.

One day, the sunrise wasted behind a grey drizzle, he found the shed door ajar. When he stepped into the damp dimness, a force knocked him against the doorframe, and a rough wetness streaked across his cheek. He struck out with his hands, pushed his fingers into fur. "Get away!" he cried and stumbled out into the yard.

A dog followed, rose to its hind legs, and planted its paws against the man's chest. Mr. Buckler forced it off with his forearm and looked down to the muddy splotches on his shirt. The dog sat at his feet, tail thumping the ground.

Old and arthritic, it badly needed a bath. Straw clung to its shaggy coat, the fur matted with caked dung from the pasture. Its pupils were hazed over with thick, yellowed cataracts.

The creature followed eagerly as Mr. Buckler shrank away and cursed it, coming closer even as the man knelt with great pain to pick up a handful of stones and began throwing as hard as he could. When one struck its side with a loud thump, the dog turned slowly and retreated back toward the shed, then, as stone after stone rang against the wooden door, slunk out to the street.

———————————

That afternoon Mr. Buckler described the dog to Mr. Carey when they met in the village shop. Mr. Carey was a farmer who had lived there all his life, a rugged man with thick arms and a tan bald head whom people sought whenever there was a problem to be solved.

"That'll be Ben," Mr. Carey said. "He hasn't been seen in months. Since before the time you arrived. I wonder what brings him back."

"Who does he belong to?" Mr. Buckler asked, ready to tell the owner to keep the animal chained.

"Ben?" Mr. Carey laughed. "He belongs to himself."

Ben, Mr. Buckler learned, roamed the village, sleeping in sheds, in hay stacks, under the stars, eating scraps tossed when villagers thought of it, rooting through garbage when they didn't.

"He's the ugliest animal I've ever seen," Mr. Buckler said.

"I suppose he's that."

"Will he go away again?"

"Can't say. Ben's got a mind of his own."

Mr. Buckler resolved to forbid the dog his garden.

The next day, his spine too rigid for sitting, he kept edging along the walls from front to side to back of the cottage, leaning against window frames to spy a sight of the dog. While he stood watch at the front, he heard a whining from the back and stumbled through the two rooms just in time to see a neighbor's angry gander pursue Ben with flapping wings. The dog wanted to run but could only hop on arthritic hindquarters. The gander gave up at the property line when Ben crawled through the bushes into the pasture.

Smiling with satisfaction, Mr. Buckler brewed himself a pot of tea.

The village was just a dozen dwellings spread haphazardly along twisting dirt lanes, its center a grassy triangle with a mailbox and a red telephone kiosk outlined against the distant hills. Mr. Buckler was clutching the receiver with a fistful of coins, trying to discuss his disability payments with an uncomprehending government clerk, when Mr. Carey drove his cows from the pasture to their sheds, the kiosk directly in their path. Quickly, Mr. Buckler squeezed inside and pulled the door tight, fearful of being trampled beneath their great dumb bulk. But the cows only lumbered by, rubbing flanks against the glass. Mr. Carey followed behind the last cow, striding in black wellies that came above his knees, prodding the animals with a long stick, Ben beside him, paws sinking into the mud of the hoof tracks. Mr. Carey saluted with a twig to his cap and nodded to Mr. Buckler.

Despite the disability award, Mr. Buckler's accident wasn't fully the factory's fault, but partly the result of his annoyance at a task undone, of his frustration at the skinny arms and sunken chest that denied him the other men's strength for heavy lifting.

For thirty years, from the time he left school at fifteen, each morning he had squeezed through rows of great clanking machinery into a dusty cubicle where he sorted rumpled sheets of paper from one pile to another, scratching in numbers with a stub of pencil.

One afternoon, when a shipment fell far behind schedule while the others sat amid the piles of boxes smoking and laughing, he hurried from his cubicle and began carrying cartons from here to there, straining against the weight, drenched in sweat. Then he stooped to lift again and screamed with pain, as if someone had driven a spike into the small of his back. He dropped the carton and crushed two toes. But they healed. It was three vertebrae that were beyond repair.

And now, he told himself when he remembered that agony, he had a peacock in his garden.

It was mating season. The peacock shrieked half the night now. Mr. Buckler lay awake sprawled flat on the hard mattress, eyes burning with fatigue. Toward morning he would doze in fitful exhaustion and then snap wide awake at the first loud cry, no more rested than he had been the previous evening

Because he did not bend where a man should, he needed an elaborate pulley contraption bolted to the ceiling beams to lift himself out of bed, gripping the hand rings that dangled over his chest and drawing himself up against the resistance of lead weights.

Feet on the floor, Mr. Buckler would splash water on his face, rub a damp cloth in his eyes, and await another day.

Every evening Mr. Carey, after his hours in the fields, strode about the village, without a break in his step unless he met one of his neighbors for conversation. Ben began following him, starting at his side but, unable to keep pace, drifting further and further back until Mr. Carey stopped to visit and the dog could creep up and crouch in the tall grass, poised for the man's next movement. Mr. Buckler had taken to watching the path that would take Mr. Carey past his doorway, shifting impatiently while the man said the same things to the same people, talk of harvests and beasts.

Finally in the grey twilight, Mr. Buckler confronted Mr. Carey, gripping the fence to step out into the lane just as the man approached with Ben hobbling at his side, panting a long flapping tongue.

"Are you feeding that dog, Carey?"

"Now and again. Ben does no harm"

"He's been after the geese."

"Ben? He couldn't stand up to a hummingbird."

———————————

The village peahens paid no attention to the peacock, one more indifferent than the next. Nothing he could think to do, no matter how spectacular his performance, interested them. They luxuriated on fence posts, with elegant small crown-combed heads and plump white bodies.

The peacock fixed himself in the middle of the yard and fanned his plumage into an arc that seemed ten-feet wide, a blaze of colors. Then his body turned a slow circle and his brown tail feathers shimmered as he emitted screams of passion. Mr. Buckler stared fascinated from a window while the hens took no notice.

———————————

There had been a Mrs. Buckler, the pale, scrawny girl whose machine he had passed each morning as he crossed the factory floor. They were both seventeen when they married. For all their years together, he never could forget the desperation in her eyes on their wedding day. He had expected her to cry out and bolt for escape, what he would have done if he had known where to turn once he left the chapel door.

Along the way she had become a shriveled woman with bad teeth, who one day just drifted off, never returning from a visit with the children to her family. For a week he kept expecting the door to open and the silent faces to enter the room. Then he stopped waiting. Although he had the address, he never wrote.

Four of them had been cramped into a cottage so small he could stretch out both arms and touch the side walls. They had a view of a slagheap and dingy washing that always hung across the tiny cinder yards. All night he could hear the neighbor's hacking cough, his gurgling phlegm. It was better to be alone.

———————————

"I'm holding you responsible, Carey," Mr. Buckler said, when he met the man outside the shop.

"What on earth for?"

"That dog."

"What's he done, Buckler?"

"He's a blight on the village. I can't stand the sight of him."

"All you have to say is 'Ben, go home,' and he'll be gone in a minute."

"He won't listen to me."

"I'll show you how it's done."

And that evening during his walk Mr. Carey demonstrated. He strode down the path, the dog came up, and they met outside Mr. Buckler's cottage. "Ben, go home," Mr. Carey said. The dog's tail drooped between legs and he disappeared into the weeds. Mr. Buckler watched through the rest of Mr. Carey's rounds. But the man walked alone the whole time.

———————————

Near midnight, after an hour of staring at the shadows on the ceiling, Mr. Buckler pulled himself from the bed, drew on his trousers, and stepped barefoot out into his yard to see if the moon would appear from behind the clouds. There, atop the chimney, the peacock perched silhouetted against an ebony sky.

"Come down from there," Mr. Buckler hissed, as though the creature were doing something foolish. "You'll break your neck."

Something warm brushed his hand. He almost cried out but

inhaled the odor of stale manure and knew it was Ben.

"Get away!" he threatened.

Ben moved off only slightly until his shape was a grey blur in the darkness. Mr. Buckler could hear the rasp of his breathing.

He dropped to his knees and groped among the rocks that lined the path, then grasped a tree trunk to pull himself up, shifting a rock from hand to hand. He moved toward the blur and held the rock above his head, counting slowly without any idea of the number that was his goal. The clouds parted slightly, and a haze of moonlight reflected from the blank eyes that gazed up at him. The dog rolled on its back and whimpered. With a shudder, Mr. Buckler dropped the rock. When he looked up again, the peacock was gone from the chimney.

———————————

Mr. Buckler no longer slept. Night after night he watched the peacock move restlessly about the garden, listened to its cries of longing. It hopped from fence to tree to ground and back again. The peahens clustered by a corner of the cottage, heads tucked against their breasts.

Ben appeared on the grass, snout to the ground, as if following a scent straight to the peacock. Mr. Buckler couldn't breathe, expecting to hear a growl, an awful shriek, the crunch of the bird's gizzard, feathers dragged through the dust.

The dog slunk in a slow circle around the bird, crouching lower and lower. The peacock lifted on its haunches, clawed at the earth, and sent a rippling through its body.

"Kill him first!" he cried to the bird. "Kill the ugly thing!"

But, with a shake of its crown, the bird folded its legs and dropped to the grass, plumage stretched out straight behind, colors shimmering in the moonlight. Tail limp, Ben crept into the shadows.

Mr. Buckler stood frozen at the window, mouth so dry he could not speak.

———————————

In the morning, pain spreading from his fingertips to his toes, Mr. Buckler fetched bread and milk from the pantry. He tore hunks of the bread into a bowl and soaked them in milk, then placed the bowl on the gravel by the cottage door. He braced himself in the doorway while Ben emerged from under the shrubs and sniffed his way to the food. The dog paused in bewilderment, then slurped greedily in the bowl.

Mr. Buckler reeled with a great emptiness as if the animal's hunger were his own.

QUEEN'S PALACE

The cornice was false. Because he craved perfection Philip noticed it at once with his eye for blemishes. He touched Hallie on the shoulder and pointed to the line where wall met ceiling. Instead of geometrical relief, a shadow had been painted to give the illusion of three dimensions. The effect may have been convincing on an 18th century evening with the huge room illuminated by flickering candles. But it was ludicrous by daylight. Surely any queen would have known. Amid the gowns and jewels and chamber strings, she had only to glance upward to know the fraud of her elegance.

———————

"Not much grandeur here," Philip told Hallie.

The girl slid the sole of one shoe along the gleaming parquet floor. "Then why did we come?"

"I'm a seeker of beautiful places. Now I know this isn't one I might have missed."

"It's ok. Better than our house. We don't have paintings and crystal chandeliers and fancy furniture."

"But the paintings are second rate. The furniture's top-heavy. It's a tacky palace."

"It's still a palace."

———————

Philip followed his daughter through a doorway. The parquet ended abruptly as he passed into a dim unfinished chamber with rough wide planking that sagged under his step.

"Look at this," he said. "A queen should have the best."

"A queen's just a woman."

"We need special people," he insisted.

———————

Hallie lingered at a window to look out toward a man-made lake that glittered in the afternoon sun.

"What do you think?" Philip asked.

"It's pretty," she said. "Very peaceful."

"Compared to Versailles? Or Blenheim?"

"They're different."

"When the great palaces were being built, the Swedes were too poor for magnificence."

"That wasn't their fault. They did the best they could."

———————

Golden-framed portraits of women lined the walls. Queens, princesses, duchesses. Pale, long-nosed, thin-lipped women with beauty spots on their cheeks and white hair puffed beneath brilliant tiaras.

For a moment Philip could not help picturing his wife, Hallie's mother, at her mirror, in an old prom gown, rings on each finger, broaches scattered over her lacy bodice, a tangle of beads and necklaces wrapped around her throat. Caked mascara filled the hollows her her eyes; orange rouge smeared down one side of her face. Very slowly she wiped a lipstick over her mouth and continued a line across her jaw onto a bare shoulder. "I'm making myself lovely for Philip," she crooned, unaware of his reflection directly behind her own in the mirror. Quickly he clenched his fists and forced her out of his memory.

———————

Philip pointed out the portrait of a full-length queen to Hallie, a silver-gowned woman surrounded by ribboned lap dogs and ruffled children. "Wouldn't you like to be special?"

"I just want to be myself."

"I suppose in our family that's an achievement."

She moved away from him pretending to examine a vase.

Leaving the red-faced Germans across the room, the guide shifted to impeccable English as she approached Philip and Hallie with more history of the palace. The heroic prince in the painting looked like an imbecile to Philip because the artist had placed his eyes at two different levels. But the guide was another Scandinavian beauty. Her smile dazzled. Yet even her flawlessness disappointed. Philip sensed no warmth about her, no response of masculine yearning in himself. But then he had stopped desiring women long before this trip.

"I hear the theater's great," Hallie said to the guide, surprising Philip with the knowledge.

The woman, much taller, smiled down at her. "It is wonderful. But I'm afraid it is not open now."

Hallie turned tightlipped, Philip unsure whether the cause was not seeing the theater or failing in her attempt to share an interest with him.

She was a pretty girl, petite, with thick waves of brown hair and the soft eyes her mother had when she was young and sound. He wished her nose were not quite as broad, her mouth wider. With only the slightest modifications she would have been stunning.

On the pebbled path, Philip took Hallie's arm to lead her toward the theater. "We can look at the outside. Maybe peek in a window."

She slipped free of his hand. "It doesn't matter." Philip saw she was about to sulk and promised himself that he would not become angry.

"There are other things we can do," he offered.

"Why did we ever come on this trip anyway?"

"To get you away from rock records and junk food."

"Really, why?"

"The magic of the north. Scandinavia. Its forests and fjords. The midnight sun. The welfare state."

"You're not being serious."

"Can't a man like being a tourist? What other reason would I have?"

"The real one."

They walked the grounds in silence, Philip unable to hold his daughter and finally speak of her confined mother. He had hoped a new place would matter. But so far it had not helped to be away from their house, from the limp dresses in the closet, the jumble of leaking cosmetics in the medicine chest, the incoherent collect phone calls.

Philip scooped a handful of pebbles from the path and tried to scale them across the surface of the lake. But each one fell heavily and sank. When he offered pebbles to Hallie, she shook her head.

"At fourteen you've seen more of the world than most people ever will."

"You make it sound so important." Hallie sighed, at the edge of exasperation.

"Don't you care about seeing things? Knowing things?"

"There are things I'd like not to know."

Philip was tempted to stop their walking and ask what things. But his nerve failed. "If not travel, what is important to you?"

"Being like everybody else."

"But you're better."

"It's enough to be ordinary."

"For God's sake, why?"

"Can't you see? Don't you understand?" Her voice was about to collapse. If he reached out to her, she would burst into tears. But he was afraid to know her misery, and so pointed out architecture, a cupola, the sweep of a railing.

"Could you eat something?"

Hallie nodded.

Philip tried teasing. "I won't have to force you?"

"No. I'm hungry enough."

Far from the palace, out on the broad lawn along the drive from the gates to the highway, was a restaurant with chairs and tables spread over the grass. Philip ordered a plate of pickled salmon, Hallie a hamburger.

"This is the life," he said. "Bright sun. A blue sky. Good food. A pretty girl."

"You'll probably find a bone."

"In the fish or in the girl?"

She didn't laugh. "You always find something."

"I don't want it that way. Things turn up. They just happen."

The defectives appeared from a van driven to a space beside the restaurant building. Attendants, two men and two women, blond and handsome in white nylon uniforms, helped the creatures to the ground, guided them to tables. All seemed young, adolescents; but it was difficult to estimate ages with this collection of hunchbacks, hydrocephalics, palsied idiots. Some in braces, a few neckless, chinless, one stunted female tottering on bandy legs with great bald patches of scalp. Their teeth were awful, growing at jagged angles like mouths full of broken crockery. A skeleton thin girl slumped in a wheelchair emitted an unending wail. The attendants tried to feed them, but the food ran down their necks, splattered their bibs.

Philip fought an impulse to run, to throw money on the table and get away as fast as possible. He had barely begun his meal yet could not chew another bite. He looked down at his plate so that he would not have to see. Hallie's hand trembled on the tabletop.

He covered it with his own and whispered. "It's ok, baby. They have a right to be out in the world. They're people too," he added but did not believe a word of it.

"Is this what you brought me here to see?" Her eyes were furious.

"How could I have known? I came to find something special."

"I'll never forget this." Hallie stared out at the defectives.

Philip would not follow her gaze. He stood with his back to the other tables and tried to make his daughter leave. "Come away," he pleaded. But she sat stiffly in the metal chair, clasped the arm rungs with both hands, and forced herself to look.

"Honey, they have nothing to do with you."

"If I were a queen, these would be my subjects. That's how I'm special!"

He shook his head helplessly and tried to imagine something beautiful.

BLACK HOLE

The cloud cover thickened just as the cable car began its ascent, lifting off from the wooden boarding shed and skimming the tall spruces on the mountainside. Paul knew they had lost the sun for the day; only a small circle of blue sky remained far in the distance. When they reached the peak, even the nearby ranges would be swallowed in grey.

"We won't see a goddamn thing." Paul kicked his boot at the side of the car.

"Stop pouting," Leslie told him.

"I came here for mountains."

Their eyes locked, and Paul quivered with resentment. An hour before, maids clattering outside their hotel room, they had thrashed in lovemaking, not caring that their cries could be heard in the hallway. Now he found her lips thin and mean as she clenched her jaw. We're only good in the dark, he wanted to tell her but instead turned away from her face.

Below the dangling car, the village and its lake shrank into postcard perspective. But the plastic windows of the car were yellowed and scratched, blurring his view.

Perhaps most people had known clouds would ruin the midday brightness. Only a few others were in the car with them, pressed against the sides and peering outward: a very old man in hiking breeches with a gnarled walking stick; a mother and young daughter with the same plump, sullen face, side by side but saying nothing to each other; a middle-aged couple in shorts and thick boots over heavy woolen socks, their legs tanned and muscled.

When the car reached the first of the towering pylons that braced the cable, it rumbled over the metal base and pitched sideways. Paul panicked: the wires were snapping, they would plummet. He gripped a handrail and then—an instant later—felt foolish, wondering if Leslie had noticed. She stared out at the treetops.

"The top of the world," he scoffed.

Leslie turned to meet his gaze. "I'm as disappointed as you are."

"Seh!" The woman in shorts called out to her husband, then pointed out at the trees below. The two of them broke into a grin, the man pointing too.

"What is it?" Paul tried to follow the direction of their fingers, seeing nothing. But the others in the car were excited. The old man leaned forward on his stick. "Steinbock," he muttered. The mother and daughter began talking in urgent whispers.

"There!" Leslie tugged at Paul's sleeve. "On that ledge."

"What? Where?" Then he saw the great sweep of horns, the brown body of an animal. Now two. Perhaps three or four. Just for an instant on a promontory of rock jutting out six thousand feet above the valley. Then they were gone, plunging back into the trees.

"How many did you count?" Leslie asked him.

"I don't know. It was all so sudden."

The couple in shorts were still smiling, as if they had just enjoyed a rare treat. They spoke enthusiastically, but neither Paul nor Leslie could comprehend their German.

"I guess that was special," Leslie said.

"I barely saw a thing." Paul resented her pleasure, the picture she would carry from this spoiled day.

The car reached its final pylon, then leveled off and edged slowly into a wooden shed at the mountaintop. Paul looked back but could barely make out the lake far beneath them. The old man pushed through the door first, digging his stick into the plank flooring as if on an urgent journey.

Immediately outside the shed was a skiers' hotel with windows shuttered for the summer and, across the way, a cafe surrounded by an open deck that faced the distant ranges. It too seemed closed, but Paul noticed a figure moving behind a window.

Where the footpath began, a panoramic map named the peaks now shrouded in mist.

"Is it worth taking pictures?" Leslie said.

"Of what? Layers of grey?"

"The clouds are interesting."

She unsnapped the case and aimed the lens at dark shapes across the empty space. Snap. The motor wound a frame forward. Another snap. "They'll help us remember."

"The day we didn't see the Alps."

"But we did see steinbock."

"You did. All I just got was a flash of hide."

"You live in such a disappointing world," Leslie said.

"How can you say that, my love?"

She turned away from him. "We're here. So we might as well walk."

A yellow wanderweg marker pointed directions and estimated times of journey: 3 Stunden here, 4 Stunden and 20 Minuten there.

"Let's just do a circle," Paul called to her. "There's no point in having a destination when you can't see."

He noticed the others behind them, the couple and the mother and daughter, but not the old man. At first the path was broad and open; but after a quarter mile it began to narrow and hug the rockface, the surface varying from stone to mud to snow. During a long icy stretch they had to clutch at the rough boulders for fear of sliding down an embankment. "Be careful!" Leslie warned. Her fear made his blood surge.

Paul looked out into the mist and felt his heart pounding. He wondered how far he would plunge if he let go. The grey seemed bottomless, a portal to absolute nothing. What would Leslie say if he vanished? If his hand reached out and pulled her after him?

Suddenly a cloud parted, for just a few seconds, and they glimpsed a snowcapped peak towering directly across the valley. Leslie cried out, and he stood there beside her, boots sunk in mud, trying to extract a deep memory from the moment. Then the grey swept back like a curtain closing.

Paul shook his head. "I can't stand being teased. I want to see."

"What's the point of this?" Leslie said. "Why don't we head back?"

"Let's get up to that curve first." He strode ahead, striking out as if his boot heels were wedges.

The path began to rise, at first gradually and then a steep climb. Paul found himself sweating even though the day was dank and chill. He half imagined they would round the bend and discover something wonderful, a sudden clarity that would illuminate the world around them. But they turned past a protruding edge of rock and stepped into a wall of white fog. Only shadows lay beyond. Paul thought he saw the old man with the stick outlined in the distance.

"Let's just stop," Leslie insisted.

Paul nodded and silently cursed the day. "It couldn't get any worse."

They reversed direction and followed the path back toward the cable car shed. Paul expected to meet the others who had come up to the mountain with them. Yet they encountered only three young men with loaded backpacks and pressed against the rock to let them pass. One, his expression very serious, said something long and elaborate in German. Paul nodded as if he understood.

"Maybe he was trying to warn us about something," Leslie said.

"He was lamenting the wonders we've missed."

She shook her head. "They know what they're doing. We don't."

"With us it's just one blunder after another."

Back at the cafe they chose a table on the deck. Against the opposite railing sat the mother and daughter, and two tables from them the couple in shorts. Paul needed coffee to take off the chill, impatient for someone to wait on them, until he finally pushed back the chair and went inside where a group of people worked busily in the kitchen. A shaggy, black dog sniffed his hand and curled up under a table again. Paul was puzzled by all the preparations. No other cable cars would arrive on this day. The mountaintop was almost empty. Who would they serve?

He ordered two cups of coffee to carry back out to the deck.

"How long do you want to stay?" he asked Leslie, wondering what he would do if she told him to go back alone.

"I want to sit for a while. The clouds are soothing."

"You're not serious."

"We should try to imagine what's behind them."

"Maybe there's nothing." Paul leaned sideways off his chair and peered over the deck's railing. "If we stepped out there, we'd fall over the edge."

"Of what?"

"The universe. Beneath that layer of clouds, there's a black hole swallowing anything that comes close." Paul made a loud slurping noise.

Attracted by the sound, the black dog come out onto the deck to sit at Paul's boots and slap the planks with its tail. Paul reached down to scratch its ears, but kept his eyes on Leslie. "Absolute total annihilation." He slurped again.

"It's terrible when you get this way," Leslie said.

"What way am I?"

"Weird. Still sulking over the clouds."

"You'd sulk too if you were poised over a black hole."

"I'm sitting here with you."

"A black hole is a private experience."

The dog braced its paws on Paul's knees and reached its snout up to lick his face. Paul hugged the dog and smacked a mock kiss on the top of its head. "And I love you too," he said.

Leslie stood so quickly she knocked over her chair. "I'm going back to the village."

Paul pushed the dog away and stepped after her, expecting the animal to follow. But it turned into the restaurant. Paul noticed all the tables were empty now. He hadn't seen the people get up.

When they entered the cable car shed, no one was inside. Though it was not yet evening, wooden clock hands indicated the day's final descent was ten minutes away. Paul wondered where the others were; the mountaintop had no overnight accommodations. The cable car waited beside the turnstile, the door shut tight. The operator was not in sight.

"Do you think they canceled the last trip?" Paul said.

"Why don't you call someone?"

He cupped hands to his mouth and bellowed "Helloooo," the tone waving as he turned his head from one side to the other. When no one answered, Paul stepped out from the back of the shed and found a bearded man digging in a long trench that came up to his waist.

"We"—Paul pointed to himself and back inside toward Leslie—"want to ride down."

The man dug out three more shovels full, working with a slow steady rhythm, wiped his hands on the back of his trousers, and used the shovel for leverage to climb from the hole. He gestured for Paul to follow as if annoyed at the interruption.

Inside the shed, he unlocked the car door, motioned Paul and Leslie aboard and locked it again even though it was still five minutes before the departure time on the sign. He pressed a row of four buttons one by one. Indicator lights for the first three changed from red to green, but the fourth blinked amber. The man went though the series again, then just the last button several times. The blinking continued.

He gave Paul an angry look as if the problem were his fault and stood staring at the control panel.

"What's wrong?" Leslie said.

"Black hole alert."

For an instant, Paul thought she would slap him, but she turned and walked to the opposite end of the car.

The operator unlocked a metal door beside the buttons and took out a telephone receiver, speaking German and running his fingers over the controls as if in response to instructions. The light continued to blink amber, and he shook his head. He hung up and unlocked the car door. "Kein gehen," he told Paul.

"What?"

The man shrugged. "Kaput." He broke into a sudden grin.

"What happens to us?"

The man gave him a puzzled look, thought for a moment, and began to mimic walking, standing in one spot and lifting his knees one after the other.

"This is crazy." Paul waved two slips of paper in the man's face. "We have tickets."

The man laughed.

"It's not funny. We paid for a cable car." He reached out toward the row of buttons, but the man, face suddenly grim, blocked his hand with a forearm.

"Paul!" Leslie pulled him away. "There's something wrong. It's probably dangerous."

"So what's your solution?"

"We walk. I saw a footpath on the way up."

Immediately outside the shed a yellow arrow pointed toward the village below, indicating a two-hour hike. Before they began, the operator was already back in the trench tossing shovels of dirt at the trees behind them.

The path spiraled in broad sweeping arcs that doubled backwards to make a gradual descent down the steep incline. At a plateau below the cable car shed where cattle grazed among the wildflowers, the path broadened into the width of an automobile. Paul and Leslie walked side by side, their boots crunching down on fresh tire tracks; but they saw no vehicles or people, just a few slate-roofed outbuildings and dozens of tan cows munching with lowered heads. A shallow stream followed the contours of the path, here and there cows standing in the rocky bed, switching tails, the twisting flow of water covering their hooves.

Paul mooed whenever they passed close to one of the animals.

"Leave them alone," Leslie said.

"Afraid of a charge? What would people say? Paul and Leslie gored by a Guernsey."

"I'd rather be gored than bored."

He gripped her shoulder to shove her off the path, then squeezed the wrist of the hand that lashed back. "Just saving you from the cow doo, dear." The path was littered with puddles of dung, most caked dry, but some dark and fresh.

She stopped still with her feet planted together.

"Paul and Leslie," he said as if addressing an audience. "They expected to have their spirits soar with the peaks. But all they found was cow shit."

"But they didn't have to come all this way to discover manure," she said.

"That's it, my love. You're getting into the spirit of the day."

They walked carefully to avoid the dung, fixing their eyes on the path, stepping around onto the grass. When they reached the trees at the end of the field, the path suddenly narrowed into a rock-strewn trail and, at several spots, almost disappeared. They had to choose which direction to follow, which way was the actual path and which a random line of bare ground.

The descent turned arduous. They gripped roots and branches not to lose their footing. As the tree cover thickened, they moved from pale haze into darkness. In the shadow, the temperature dropped to what felt like twenty degrees. Paul rolled down his sleeves, and Leslie buttoned her collar.

She tripped on a rock and landed on her hands and knees in a bed of damp moss. Paul thought she might cry, but she pulled herself up and sat back against a tree.

He watched for a moment and then decided to kneel beside her. "You OK?"

"I stunned myself."

He leaned across, took her chin in his hand to kiss her, intending a mocking touch of lips, but pressing hard, feeling the shape of her teeth. She sank against him, and he wondered what to do next, how far she expected him to go. Then he heard footsteps.

Leslie pulled away. "What was that?"

They heard more steps, loud and clear, a heavy trudging, the cracking of twigs. Paul saw a dark shape, perhaps two, fifty yards ahead. "There!" He pointed.

"I didn't see," she said.

Paul held her absolutely still and was sure he heard another sound. "Now I see something," she said, excited, standing and leaning forward into the shadows.

"What was it?"

"I don't know."

"How many?"

"I couldn't be sure. It was just movement."

"A steinbock?" he said, not certain if he should make it a joke.

She took him seriously. "It wasn't that big. What other animals do they have here?"

"It didn't sound like an animal. It may have been the couple."

"What couple?" she said.

"The people in shorts. They looked like the type who'd walk down. Should I call to them?"

She pressed her hand to his mouth. "No."

"Why not? They seemed friendly enough."

"What if it wasn't them?"

Paul thought she was joking, until he saw her eyes. Her fright excited him with possibility. "Do you think we're in danger?"

She shook her head. "I don't know. It's so odd here."

He held himself still and breathed in a damp vegetable odor, heard the distant rush of a waterfall deep in the trees. "So what do we do now? Just stand and tremble?"

"Keep heading for the village. We don't have a choice."

Paul took long strides on the brown strip of path, his boots sinking into the soft earth with each step. Right behind him he could hear Leslie panting, inhaling with great gulps. But he didn't slow down, wouldn't until she pleaded with him.

He imagined stopping abruptly, twisting his face into a hideous mask, and suddenly turning upon her with a roar. Would she scream? Faint? The victim could die of heart failure. It would be a foolproof way to get rid of a wife—if the wife had a weak heart and you wanted to get rid of her. That would be the most important thing to know—how much you really wanted her out of your life.

The wife murderer would begin running down the mountainside, stumbling off the path many times until his clothes were torn, his hands and face bleeding. He would call for help, distraught, irrational. When he finally encountered people, he would cry out "My wife! Meine Frau!" and babble incoherently. Or another type of man might drag the body deep into the woods, wedge it into a cavity in the rocks, cover it with layers of branches and dead leaves. He would burn her passport, perhaps his own, turn away from the village in a totally opposite direction and disappear into another life.

"Please," Leslie finally said, breathless, face slick with a chill sweat. "I can't keep up."

"You're the one so eager to get away from this place."

"I have to rest." She sank against a tree.

Paul reached down to pick up a thick branch at his feet. It was waterlogged, crumbling when he lifted it over his head. The roar of the waterfall was loud now. He could make it out through the trees, spirals of white plunging from the cliff above, exploding into a rocky current. "Look." He pointed, imagining how it would feel to be swept over the edge: a great ripping pain, a crush of bone, and then nothing.

At first Paul thought the scream belonged to his fantasy, a piercing cry that lasted only a few seconds and then wavered in an echo. But Leslie seized his arm. "What was that?"

"He threw her over the edge," he said.

"What! Who did?"

"The man in shorts. His wife."

She backed away from him. "Don't! That was a scream."

"Or a bird. Maybe an animal. The mating cry of the steinbock."

"Someone's in trouble. Terribly hurt."

He wasn't sure. "Where? Which way should we go?"

"I can't tell where the noise came from."

"Then let's just follow the path until we see something."

Several yards ahead they had to clutch at a great rock that blocked the way, the footing no wider that the soles of their boots, a steep drop into a pool of grey water below them. Paul peered down for the signs of a body but saw only trees reflected in the still surface.

When they rounded a bend, the woods suddenly stopped and they found themselves in a clearing staring directly at the falls. From their previous angle through the leaves, he hadn't realized how wide it was, how deep it plunged. "No one could survive," he said.

Leslie wrapped her arms around her chest and shivered. "I'm so cold."

"It's the falls—like a gigantic icicle. We'd better keep moving."

Now the path followed the edge of a valley, a hundred feet above the rushing stream. In the haze they could barely make out the hill shapes across the narrow valley. Paul had no way of knowing how far they were from the village.

A roll of thunder sounded, faint, as if many miles away. But the sky before them cracked with lightning; rain splattered the leaves. Paul pulled his shirt over his head, exposing his back to the chill, wet wind. "Can you run?" he shouted over the roar of the storm.

"It's too late." She was already drenched, strands of hair plastered to her cheeks.

Paul kept lashing out with open hands as if the raindrops were insects swarming his face. More rockface suddenly loomed in front of them. Leslie sprawled against a large boulder, arms outstretched, as if embracing it. He gripped her waist and squeezed her through a cleft into a small clearing.

There on a promontory a small square cabin of weathered logs jutted out over the valley. Large holes in the roof exposed cracked lathing; splinters of glass hung from empty window frames.

"Our lucky day," he said.

"I don't want to go in." Leslie stood rigid in the middle of the path.

Paul pushed at the cabin door. The knob just wobbled in his grip. He put his shoulder to the wood, then kicked backwards with the heels of his boots until he bent the door sideways, forcing enough space to enter.

Leslie stiffened at his hand on her arm and gripped the doorframe when he tried to push her inside.

"What the hell's the matter with you?" Furious at her resistance, he pried at her fingers, twisting them to give her pain.

When she released the wood, he heaved his weight against her, and she collapsed onto the floorboards, head buried between her knees, shaking with sobs.

Paul began coughing as soon as he followed inside. The cabin, barren except for a bleached wooden table tilted against one wall, was coated with a thick layer of dust. He kneeled beside her and seized her shoulders. But she only cried more frantically.

When he reached back to slap her, she sprawled limp on the

71

splintered wood. In an instant he was beside her, fixing her sour mouth with a fierce kiss, wriggling his body on top of hers. He expected a furious response, fists beating his back, nails digging into his flesh. But her weight was so slack he opened his eyes and found her face squeezed into a grimace, tangled hair dripping onto the wood.

"I know who screamed," she said.

"Yes?"

"It was me."

"That's crazy. I was standing right beside you. You didn't make a sound."

"I've been screaming all day."

Paul pulled away from her with an impulse to vanish into the fog. But he stopped at the doorway. Thunder roared and a new surge of storm pounded the roof, lashed through the windows. He pointed out at the thick grey haze. "The village is down below. We'll wait till the rain slows and get there by nightfall."

"It doesn't matter." Leslie huddled against the overturned table. "Wherever we go, we'll never be found."

EVAN IN THE TENT

Sunrise dazzled through the double glass of the solarium, a great orange ball hovering above the bare oaks at the far edge of the property. Miranda had to shield her eyes, squint, to make out the shape of her brother's brown tent pitched under the trees along the bank of the brook. Then a flap moved and Evan stepped out, bare-chested, stretching his arms toward the sky, surrounded by a shimmering glow. She almost smiled, reliving an old memory, but he suddenly doubled over and dropped to his knees, head hanging over the water. Though Miranda couldn't hear a sound, she knew he was retching, sick, in pain. In her thoughts she cursed her stepfather for refusing to let Evan inside the house, for screaming that he wanted her brother out of his life, and she cursed her mother for not fighting back.

Miranda knew she could slide open the glass door and step on the soft grass, hurry out past flower beds now dry with winter, and embrace Evan, wrap her arms around him to still his tremors. But she couldn't make herself move, remembering how yesterday he had shaken her off, his voice a snarl: "It's not your problem." She had sat on the ground beside him and wept, Evan refusing to look at her, slapping the food she brought from her hands and throwing it into the brook. She had watched the soft current carry off slices of bread that vanished behind thick yews.

A house of four-thousand square feet, twelve rooms, four bathrooms, and her stepfather wouldn't even let Evan inside to use the toilet. "He married me, not an addict," her mother had told Miranda, whispering the words. And Charles, the man who had replaced her father, shouted behind closed doors: "It's bad enough we've got her and her kid. When are you going to get rid of him?"

Children of privilege, brother and sister, now adults in their thirties, were back to the home of their childhood, the one Charles took over after he married their mother, insisting on replacing the furniture, redecorating, removing all signs of their father, making it his.

Evan hadn't been invited to the yard, hadn't asked permission. Two days ago, three weeks after she left Brad and brought Joseph with a box of his toys and a car full of suitcases, Miranda saw the tent, army surplus, sagging in the middle, ropes in a tangle of stakes. She knew at once it was her brother, though she hadn't heard from him in months, had lost track since he stopped checking in and out of one rehab facility after another, disappearing in just a few nights, their desperate mother having no idea where he was until the next center called.

"Who's that man?" Joseph had asked the day Evan appeared, pointing out at the shape by the tent, face scrunched in six-year-old puzzlement. Miranda's mother just shook her head, but Miranda said, "That's my brother. Your uncle." The boy wanted to know why he was there, why he wasn't inside with them. "Because he's sick, very sick," Miranda told him. And her mother had fled the room.

Evan got down on all fours, wriggling toward the brook, hanging his head over the bank until the chill current rushed over his face. He opened his mouth to gulp water, swish it about to clear the taste of vomit. The brook was so cold it stung, but he couldn't make himself pull back, as if his existence were nothing but this sense of hurt. Then he had to breathe, sucked in a nose full of water and rolled to his back, gagging and sputtering. It must have looked funny, he told himself, when he was able to sit up, though he didn't laugh.

Frost clung to the grass blades, a silvery coat that reflected the sun. Evan ran an open hand over the tips, clearing streaks of green, swooping in circles, slashing straight lines, fascinated by the patterns that appeared. He stopped abruptly, his stomach aching with great hunger. He ripped up fistfuls of grass and stuffed them into his mouth, chewing madly, smearing dirt across his lips, over his cheeks.

Shivering, he crept back inside the tent, pulled a shirt over his shoulders, rolled over inside a blanket until he was wrapped in layers. A brown paper bag lay just beyond his fingertips, filled with vials of pills that he had taken from his father's office. He barely remembered bursting into the office, insisting to the receptionist that he had to see his father, being told his father was with a patient, then pushing his way into an empty treatment room and smashing the lock of a cabinet with rows of medications lined behind glass doors. He had seized handfuls, stuffing them into his pockets, running when he heard his father cry his name, knocking the receptionist off her feet, tripping out the door onto the street.

Now he reached into the bag to grab the first vial he touched. He popped off the plastic lid with his thumb and slid out two pills, swallowing them, not knowing which they were, not caring. He lay on his back and watched the pinpricks of sunlight at the stitching of the tent until his head spun.

———————————

Ellen would not look, kept the kitchen window blinds shut day and night, stayed away from the back of the house, trying to pretend her son was not living in a tent two hundred feet away. When his father called about the stolen pills, she pressed the mute button and hummed a tune to herself. She knew he wouldn't turn their son in to the police, didn't want their names in the newspapers, the bad publicity.

His voice had been calm, had always been that way, his typical refusal to admit how upset he was. Now she lived with a man, Charles, who never held back, shouting his fury, shouting when she told him Miranda had left her husband, that she and Joseph would be living with them until she established a new life. He had pounded a tabletop, ranting what a mess her children had made of their lives. But she had stood her ground, reminded him she had left their father to be with him. Charles could have said, what about your son? Were you a drug addict too? But he never did, never went that far, rarely mentioning Evan's name. She expected him to call the police when the tent appeared in the yard, yet all he said was, "Never let him inside this house." And, though she would not admit it to him, she agreed, relieved that she would not have to be in the same room with her son, not have to relive the years of confrontations, the slammed doors that knocked china off the shelves, the objects that were missing every time he left a room.

When her first husband, the doctor, on the phone, started telling her again that Evan had never been on drugs during their marriage, how it all started when Charles came into her life, she had pressed the off button and stared at the silent phone.

Ellen would not say anything about the pills to Miranda. They were together all day, pretending to watch television, an excuse not to talk. When Miranda first told her about the tent in the yard, she shook her head and insisted that she didn't want to know, that Miranda was to report nothing, that her grandson was to know nothing. "If you ever mention your brother, you'll have to leave this house," she had said, stunned by the words coming out of her mouth.

———————————

The doctor shut the door to his private office, tugging the knob to make certain it was closed, then lifted the telephone and poised a finger over the speed dial number. Miranda had left a message about Evan's tent, crying, choking on her words, pleading. But what would he say to his daughter? Every time he tried to help his son, he ended up reeling, as if a fist had punched him in the stomach. But he knew once he heard Miranda's voice, he would give in and agree to find a place for Evan. He turned to the framed print on his wall, a Monet that always soothed him with its shimmering greens. Reaching behind him, studying the painting, the doctor set down the phone and awaited the signal for his next patient.

———————————

When he stopped hugging his stuffed dog and stepped out of his bed, Joseph went directly to the window, as he did for hours since the man his mother called his uncle had appeared in the yard. He would stand and stare, his nose almost touching the glass pane, until his mother called his name.

He had wanted a room next to hers, the way it had been in their house. But this house wasn't like that. The rooms on both sides of his mother's, the one that had been hers when she was his age, were used by other people, one to sleep in and one for the office of the man his mother told him to call Grandma's husband. His mother had wanted him to sleep with her, but that man had said no, his face red and twisted. Joseph knew grownup's anger, the way his mother and father had shouted at each other. This was louder and worse, frightening him, making him cry. The man said he had to sleep in the small room at the end of the hallway, the one no person had ever used before. His grandmother had told him that as if it surprised her to remember.

Other than a picture of a sailboat hung on one wall, the room was barren, no books on the shelves, just a narrow bed, a dresser now filled with his clothes, and a desk with empty drawers under the window. Joseph would lean over that desk while he watched, seeing lumps in the tent that told him someone was moving, then the front flaps part and an arm reach out and pull back quickly. At times, not very often, his uncle would slide out onto the grass and just sit there, his legs crossed in front of him, his face in his hands. Joseph would barely breathe when he was like that, barely move. Once his uncle had toppled forward, face flat on the ground for a very long time, until he rose to his knees and dragged himself back inside the tent.

This morning when he saw his uncle's head in the water, he thought his uncle was going to drown, imagining a body being swept away around the bend of the narrow brook, even though he knew the water was only inches deep. He wanted to rush to his mother and warn her about what was happening. But he feared she would scold him because he had been told to have nothing to do with his uncle, never to go out into the yard. His grandmother had nodded all the time his mother was telling him about that rule, then repeated it almost word for word when his mother finished. His grandmother would scold him too, the man who was her husband shout at him. But if his uncle drowned, he would blame himself, even if he never let anyone else know what he had seen.

When his uncle rolled over and sat up, when he spat mouthfuls of water, when he rubbed dirt on his face, Joseph cried out his relief—

"Oh!" —then waited for footsteps in the hallway, certain he had done something wrong, waiting to be punished.

Miranda tried to read, sunk into a soft chair in the house's great room, an open book face down in her lap, but she stared at the flames dancing about the false logs in the gas fireplace. The pictures were gone from the bookshelves. Her stepfather had seen to that, and she had no idea where to find the photographs of her family when they were all young and her mother was married to her father. Even though it was absent, she could clearly envision the largest of the pictures, she and Evan sitting cross-legged by the garden in summer, surrounded by rich blooms, the boy with his arms around his big sister's neck, his mouth open with laughter, her face bright with smiling. She knew she would never forget that photo, could barely believe it had ever been real.

Her marriage might have survived if not for her brother, the phone calls in the middle of the night, Jonathan handing her the receiver as if it were vermin, Evan incoherent, begging for money, threatening to kill himself, Jonathan signaling her to hang up with angry hand gestures. And the last time Evan pounded on their door, crying that he craved sleep, that they had to let him in. Finally, Jonathan told her, "I can't live this way." Miranda had nodded, saying nothing, knowing that there was nothing she could say, nothing she could do, no way she could stay. Her brother would always be a force in her life.

When Miranda heard the solarium door slide open and felt a chill breeze biting at her bare ankles, she called out, "Mother" and then "Joseph." No one answered. She stood up, unwillingly, annoyed, moving into the hallway, thinking she had to close it tight.

As she stepped onto the cool tile floor, she saw her son running across the garden bed, trampling the dry brown stems, heading toward the tent. And behind the tent, Evan lying full length in the middle of the brook, the current splashing over his naked body. Even from a distance she could tell how emaciated he was, legs skeletal, his chest sunken, his hair wild.

Miranda heard Joseph crying out, "Don't drown. Don't drown." She heard her mother's gasps, then felt a presence in the solarium, heavy footsteps pounding behind her. Her stepfather. She turned just as her mother tried to block him with her arms around his waist. "Charles!" He pushed her off and strode into the yard.

"He'll freeze in that water," Miranda said to her mother. "He'll freeze to death."

But Evan was on his feet, stepping up onto the bank, reaching out when Joseph rushed past the tent, grabbing the boy's forearms and swinging him back and forth. The moment Miranda thought he would tear her son's shoulders, Joseph began crying out, her mother screaming, the two of them, her son and her mother, both hysterical.

Her stepfather took a path through the tent, deliberately, stomping it flat, kicking at the cloth, all in seconds before he reached back and slapped Evan across the face again and again, until Evan dropped the boy. Joseph lay on the grass, shaking with sobs, his eyes terrified. Her stepfather was punching Evan, beating his fists into Evan's chest and stomach, lashing out in fury.

Evan made no effort to defend himself, just stood with limp arms, as if he had no idea what was happening. Her mother let out a breathless shriek. Miranda knew she should hurry to embrace her son, to stop her stepfather, to pull him off. But she did not move, rooted, frozen, shocked by her wish that a man she despised would kill her brother.

IN THE WOODS

Carl sensed the man—Pryor—would be his father even before the car stopped. Fleeing home on the pitch-dark street, the crash of glass echoing through his skull, he felt something very strange about the scarlet Charger easing along the street beside him. It moved much too slowly for the police, skewed, the trunk crushed up beneath the splintered rear window, jagged plastic where the taillight should be, the back bumper dangling as if the accident had just happened. For an instant, he felt that he had caused it, as if the rocks he had hurled had wrecked that car instead of a neighbor's sun porch. Then the car stopped and the sound of his name made him look toward the smiling young woman in the passenger's seat, and beyond her to the father he had never seen, the man's mouth grim and unwelcoming. "Get in," Pryor said, the first words Carl ever heard from him, and Carl did, as if reeled by a taut line, onto the seat beside Jacqueline the moment she opened the door.

Here, in the cabin, deep within a dark woods, it disturbed Carl to look at Pryor, as if the face he had known in the mirror all his fifteen years had suddenly caved in, eaten with deep lines around the lips, hollowed beneath the cheekbones, a puffy darkness around the eyes. His father wasn't old, still under forty, but he looked as if he had been tied to a tree through months of naked weather, shriveled by a hot sun in the summer, bleached by icy winter winds. It was like seeing into his own future and knowing the life ahead would be harrowing.

Jacqueline, short and full-bodied, an adult who had never lost her baby fat, took to dragging a chair between Carl and Pryor, climbing up and wrapping her arms around their shoulders to link the three of them. "It's like having two of you with me now," she'd say. "Identical twins."

Can't you see the difference? Carl wanted to ask her when they were alone. But he never had the nerve, sure Pryor would appear at that second, even when the car was gone and his father vanished for hours. The only thing they had in common was being tall and thin, with huge hands and feet that overburdened scrawny limbs. But Pryor was agile and coordinated, as if he had learned the secret of holding his body parts in balance, while Carl constantly tripped and banged his elbows.

"Why don't you ever go out?" Jacqueline asked Carl when some days had passed. "The trees are wonderful."

"I don't know where we are," he told her.

"You won't get lost. Keep the car in sight. You can see the paint shining through the leaves."

"I am lost." They had driven all night, eating sandwiches, not even stopping for toilets, just pissing at the side of the road. He fell asleep for what must have been several hours and woke when the car was easing down the main street of a small town, without lights, hugging the curb as if parked, the town so dark he could see no signs. Then they were speeding on a two-lane highway, Pryor cursing because he had missed a turnoff, grinding gears and squealing into reverse, swerving onto a dirt road that went on for miles deeper and deeper into the woods, startled animal eyes flashing in the headlights, until they stopped beside the cabin and Pryor slept in the car, too exhausted even to step the five paces to the front room. But Jacqueline took Carl's hand and led him inside, back into a long narrow room barely wide enough for the cot, and told him that here was where he would sleep. She had pulled his face down, kissed him on the forehead—"Welcome home"—and closed the door behind her.

"I am lost," he said again when she pretended not to have heard.

"You're with your father," she said.

"Where? What state are we in? What place is this?"

"It's better that we don't talk about that."

———————

Carl pictured how his mother must be reacting, climbing up and down the stairs through sleepless nights, brewing endless pots of coffee, snapping at the other kids, the ones Eddie—the man he used to call Dad—had really fathered, the ones he had always believed were his brother and sisters until that night a year ago when she, eyes burning with tears, admitted who he really was: "Carl, a man called the house the other day. For the first time in years, I thought—prayed—he was out of our lives. Eddie—Dad—and I decided you'd better know."

But even if she had never spoken, he would have understood everything the moment that Charger pulled alongside and he saw Pryor in the driver's seat: this is my real father.

Several months ago, she had pulled him into her room and whispered: "He called again. If you ever see a tall, gaunt man looking at you—run. Run for your life!"

Carl was sure she knew where he was now, probably imagining him kidnapped, a gun in his ribs, a gag knotted across his mouth. It would kill her to know he had gotten into that car the moment he was summoned.

———————

Pryor and Jacqueline ignored Carl most of the day, digging outside, hacking and tearing at roots and rocks. She just smiled when he asked her what they were doing, and he was afraid to question Pryor, not sure how the man would react. He imagined them digging downward, excavating deep pits, dragging great black sacks from the shadows of the trees and shoving them over the edge.

Inside, not washing, just rubbing their hands on a rag of toweling nailed to the wall, the two of them would close a door for hushed conversations whose hissed urgency pierced the cabin.

Now and then Pryor left the property, thumping the car down the rutted dirt tracks through the trees, and all the time he was gone Jacqueline moved from window to window staring anxiously at the trees.

"Who owns this?" Carl asked her.

"Owns what?"

"All this place." He pointed at the dark wooden walls spotted with chinks of daylight, at the plank door, at the blur of shaded green outside the narrow glass panes. "People let us use what's theirs. We don't own a thing."

"What about the car?"

Jacqueline shook her head.

"It's wrecked."

"It runs. That's all we need."

"But you bashed up somebody's car."

"They won't mind."

"I would," he said.

"Because you let things be important."

"What's important to you?" he asked her.

"That's a secret." She smiled and wrapped her arms around him, so hard he could feel her breasts quivering against his midsection.

For the first hour in the Charger, before she climbed over into the back, they had been crushed together on the bucket seat, he thinking only of her warmth against his side even though he knew his life would never be the same.

———————————

When his mother told him, it was as if her words had lanced a pressure festering in his brain. The release rushed through his blood; he had to grip a chair to keep from swooning. Now he knew why he felt so totally different from anyone else, the sisters and brother who were so much at ease with their lives. Alone in his room, the others all together, some force inside him had made him want to smash everything—rip the posters from the walls, tear his clothing, slash at his mattress with a sharp blade. Some nights, unable to stop himself, he would rush out into the street to destroy, gouge long scratches into the neighbors' cars, uproot shrubbery, heave rocks through windows of empty rooms. Then he would huddle into the trees, trembling with a stranger's rage when police lights flashed.

———————————

Pryor away, Jacqueline sleeping behind a closed door, Carl pulled his sweater around his chest and shivered in the damp chill of the cabin. He tiptoed across the room to the door, hesitantly, waiting until each creak faded before he took another step, and then opened the door. Pausing in the doorway, he thought of his mother's housecat, a creature constantly perched on windowsills, yet terrified of the outdoors.

He made himself move into the clearing and circle the cabin, focusing his eyes on the wood, and realizing how shabbily it was constructed, bent and rusted nails, split boards, as if whoever made this place had rushed through an unwanted obligation.

It took an effort for Carl to turn toward the dense shadows of the trees. He tried to see through the thickness of the leaves and branches to a circle of clear light. But whichever way he looked the shadows deepened into total darkness.

He hurried back inside and peered down at the floorboards, waiting for Jacqueline to awake.

———————————

At home, with his mother and Eddie and the kids, there seemed to be nothing they couldn't have. The house sat on several sprawling acres of open contoured lawn, Eddie constantly adding new wings every time one of them had a wish for a game room or an indoor pool or a place for Chip to practice his drums. "Are we rich?" he remembered Melanie asking their mother, and eight-year-old Patti fascinated with the question, repeating it at least once a day. Their mother would always answer, "Comfortable," patient, as if it was the first time she had been asked.

Eddie—back in the time when Carl still thought of him as Dad— had promised him a new car when he got his license, but Carl, although he had never driven, at fourteen, took Eddie's new Lincoln for a 5 a.m. ride through the twisting streets around their house. Confused by the power steering, he lurched onto lawns, into trees, skidded against the Belgian block curbing, flattening both front tires and returning to their driveway on clanking rims. He had expected Eddie to beat him, but the man just stood there with tears streaming down his face.

Here, through sleepless nights, staring at the darkness and flinching at sudden bird screeches, he wondered what it meant to say Pryor was his real father. Was living like this, in a cabin heaped like a pile of scrap in the middle of nowhere, more real than his room in a house where every object had a private meaning? What if he had run as fast as he could at the sight of that smashed car? Did anything he did have the power to change what he was?

"Who is he?"

"Who is who?" Jacqueline said.

Carl never knew what to say: my father, Pryor. "You know. Him."

"He's your father."

"Not until last week."

"He wanted to be. Very much."

"Is that what he says?"

"He was never able to come for you before."

"Why? Where was he?" Carl asked.

"Far. A world away. He risked everything to be here."

"To get me?"

"It's all part of something very important." Jacqueline clasped both his hands between hers.

"He hardly ever talks to me."

"What he's doing takes all his concentration. All his energy."

"Then why didn't he wait and get me when it's over?"

"You're the only son he has."

"Why does he need a son now?"

"He wants to save you." She spoke with urgency, her eyes glistening.

"From what?"

"From what's going to happen." The way she said it made him shudder.

Carl looked to the door that separated them from Pryor, as if he could see through the wood to the man sitting clench-fisted at the table, into the man's skull where a red-hot force pulsed on the edge of explosion. "What?" Carl insisted. "Tell me what!"

"He's been waiting so long," Jacqueline whispered.

Carl shook his head, squeezed his eyes tight to stop the tears. "He scares me." But as much as he fought it, Carl found himself crying, deep heaving sobs that he hadn't known since he was a child. He slid down against a wall until he was huddled into a corner rocking back and forth. "Please don't tell him," he pleaded. "Don't ever tell him I said that."

Jacqueline was beside him, stroking his face and making soothing sounds. "You don't know. You don't know anything," she was saying, over and over.

———————

Someone—Pryor or Jacqueline—had left photographs stacked on a table, mostly scenes without people, not beautiful places, but plain houses and buildings, everything uncentered and at odd angles: a port with winches hoisting cargo over the side of a huge ship, an empty highway where stunted palms grew along a narrow dividing strip. The only photo of people had two men, one dark and shirtless, wearing a cap with a gold-braided peak. They held out drinks in one hand and wrapped their free arms around each other's shoulders. The shadow of a palm tree fell across the faces and blanked out their features.

The three of them sat down to dinner at the rough plank table, barely speaking, Pryor just grunting when Jacqueline asked if this day's trip from the woods had worked out. The food was tasteless, a heated pulp poured from a can. Carl could hear their chewing, Jacqueline scratching at her dish with a fork, Pryor staring off at a spot on the wall, thinking, always thinking.

Carl dug up splinters of wood with his fingernails. He wanted one of them to tell him to stop. But it was as if they didn't care how much he destroyed. Hearing his heart thump in the silence, he summoned up the courage to speak. "What about my mother?"

Pryor looked at him and blinked, surprised someone else was in the room. He frowned at the intrusion.

"My mother," Carl insisted. "Does she know?"

"Know what?" Pryor said.

"That I'm with you."

"Of course not. Why should she know?"

"It would mean trouble," Jacqueline added, tentative.

"I don't want her to worry. She should know I'm safe."

"Your mother doesn't matter," Pryor said.

"I love her," Carl shouted, trembling at his eruption, ready to duck his head.

Pryor reached out and seized his face, clamping Carl's jaw in his long fingers. "You love knowing how much she's suffering at the loss of her boy. You want to hurt them all because you don't belong in that house."

Carl tried to speak: "That's not true." His teeth were cutting into the flesh of his mouth under Pryor's grip.

He had an image of Pryor creeping up to the house in that ruined car, flinging a bomb at the foundation, and racing away at the instant of explosion, obliterating everything he had known for fifteen years into a pit of scorched cinders.

Carl ripped loose. "I'll kill you!"

Pryor pushed back from the table and stood erect, almost rigid. Carl cringed at the dark look of his eyes. But his father turned and left the room.

———————————

Carl lay in darkness, gaze fixed on a spot through the window pane above where an edge of moon glowed through clouds. Suddenly it erupted, and it wasn't the sky but Eddie's sprawling house flared into flames, vanishing into a spiral of black smoke. He could feel the terrible heat, like a searing fever. But he didn't know where he was—inside screaming with the pain of the others, or outside crouched beside Pryor, his head full of the man's laughter.

Pryor came back from one of his trips with guns, two pistols in wooden cases, an automatic rifle in a leather sheath. He took to disassembling them on the table, down to the smallest springs, and cleaning each part with new white cloths and fluids from a row of clear unlabeled bottles. He devoted hours each day, no longer bothering to dig outside.

One afternoon Carl looked up to find his father pointing the rifle, the butt tight against his shoulder, fingers adjusting the sight, sure the man was aiming at his head. But he didn't move, wouldn't give Pryor the victory of seeing him drop to the floor. "Isn't that dangerous?" Carl finally said.

"Would I hurt you?" Pryor asked.

"I don't know what you'd do."

"That must make your life here very interesting." Pryor shifted the barrel an inch toward the left and squeezed the trigger. Carl gulped at the sharp click.

———————

Carl began noticing that Jacqueline was leaving the bathroom door cracked open. He wondered if she had always been doing it and he hadn't seen; but he didn't think so. He had been watching her movements since the beginning, her dragging the bucket of bath water from the pump to the metal tub, hunched over at the weight, two hands closed around the handle, only her bare feet showing under the long flannel robe, her flesh rippling beneath. When he once offered to help, she shook her head. Now through the opening he could hear the splash of water, watch the robe fall into a heap, glimpse an indistinct edge of nakedness. And he was certain he was meant to look.

———————

He never saw Pryor touch Jacqueline, never heard sounds of sex in the night. Not once did his father reveal a sign of passion or tenderness. Yet, Carl couldn't imagine that they weren't lovers. In the chill darkness, shivering under the blanket, he would press the pillow to his middle, clamp his thighs around it. .

———————

"Why are you here?" Carl asked. "With him?"

"Your father is a fascinating man."

"How long have you been together?"

"Not very long. Sometimes I feel it's been forever."

"Will you get married?"

Jacqueline smiled. "That's not why I'm here."

"How do you know it won't be like my mother? That he won't end up hating you too?"

She shook her head. "He doesn't hate your mother. He never even thinks about her."

"Then why did he punish her?"

"How?"

"By taking me."

"He didn't take you. You chose to come."

"He made me get in that car. You both did. I wouldn't hurt her."

"Carl, you're lying to yourself."

"Shut up!" He was shifting back and forth, squeezing one hand over the other. "Don't you talk about my mother."

"Carl, all I did was open a door."

He lashed out, and Jacqueline grabbed his arms, holding them stiff with surprising strength while he yanked and tugged, she smiling all the time, as if they were playing a game.

Shuddering, Carl forced her against a wall, pressing a shin into her thigh, leaning forward and flattening her breasts with his chest, humiliated by his erection. They paused panting, eyes fixed. She wasn't even angry, just annoyed, as if their struggle were only a nuisance. But he wanted her to be furious, curse his name, scream until Pryor would enter the room and hate him.

He brought his mouth down on hers, forcing his tongue against her teeth. Jacqueline squirmed a leg free and lifted a knee into his groin. Dizzy with pain, Carl fell back across the room and clamped his arms between his thighs. When he could see through the tears, she was standing above him; blurred, rearranging her hair. "I'm sorry I hurt you," she said.

"Then tell him all about it," Carl gasped. "I want him to know."

Jacqueline shook her head. "He already knows everything he has to." She left him alone in the room, writhing on the floor boards, his face against the splintered wood.

———————

Carl rolled onto his back and stared up at the roof beams, watching the shadows of late afternoon slowly swallow the light. Both Pryor and Jacqueline had gone outside. He had heard the door slam long before. He pulled himself up and moved to the window, seeing only the smashed Charger under a tree.

Carl drew back the door very slowly, with no idea what he would do if they were standing in front of the cabin. But the clearing outside was empty. He paused, unsure whether he should run or walk, which direction to choose.

He hugged the side of the building, eased around a corner to the car. Clutching the door handle, he stared at the wreck, the rear crushed, the plastic smashed, the scarlet paint gleaming like the innards of a splattered animal.

Trembling, Carl threw open the hood and tore wires from the engine, ground plastic parts under his foot, stuffed handfuls of dirt into the air filter, the radiator, and oil spout.

Then he heard the shots, first distant rifle firings, resounding cracks of explosion, and immediately after a rapid burst, nearer, that rang through his skull. He dropped to his knees and vomited, gagged and heaved phlegm, a sour burning tearing at his throat.

When he tried to stand, he pitched forward with dizziness, dropping into the bed of damp earth they had turned over with their digging. He felt wet all over but didn't dare touch himself, terrified that thick blood would ooze through his fingers. He imagined them dragging him into that ruined car, somehow making it run, driving through the night to dump his body on Eddie's doorstep, his mother's scream the last sound he would ever hear.

His name rang out, "Carl," at first in Jacqueline's voice, next shouted by Pryor, then repeated by Jacqueline, echoing from every direction; coming closer each time.

Tear-blinded, Carl reached out for a branch and pulled himself up. He swallowed and bolted into the trees, head swirling, roots tangling his shoes, branches lashing at his face. His flesh stung; pain tore through his muscles. He snagged his trousers on briars, and circles of blood spread on the cloth.

When he paused to look back through the green blur of the leaves, he saw Jacqueline and Pryor standing by the cabin, she cradling the rifle, Pryor with a pistol in each hand.

Before they could aim, Carl plunged deeper into the trees, breathless, forcing his legs through the undergrowth. But he knew there was no way out. Miles and miles of looming trees blocked the sunlight. He told himself he would run till nightfall, passing though pain into numbness, impelling himself until he collapsed. Then he would huddle in the darkness and cringe under the power of his own fear, certain no matter how far he ran that cabin would always be his home.

GYPSIES

Charles and Sylvia encountered the gypsies at the Intermarché while they waited in the checkout line with a cart of provisions for their first holiday in a landscape they had come to love from paintings—Cézannes, Monets, van Goghs. A cashier was dragging items over a scanner and shoving them down a metal shoot as customers scurried to stuff goods into plastic bags. The woman in front of them, the next customer, rocked back and forth, kicking shapeless shoes against the base of the counter, her body wide and dark in a threadbare print house dress, coarse black hair knotted in a loose braid. She carried her groceries in her hands, just three giant cans of beans and a box of sugar. Then a thin woman, haggard, her face all jaw and cheekbones, pushed a heaped cart ahead of them, goods stacked chaotically, hanging over the edges. Charles was about to cry out a protest when he saw that she was with the other woman. With that load it would be at least another fifteen minutes. He looked at Sylvia and she gave an audible sigh.

Children suddenly rushed up to the two women and hung from the sides of the cart, barefoot, the boys wearing nothing but shorts, their legs and chests streaked with mud, the girls in short, filthy dresses, shoving at each other, chattering in high-pitched voices.

Sylvia nudged Charles to look down into the cart wedged with plastic liters of cheap wine, beer, cola, prepackaged yellow cheeses, sacks of potatoes, loose heads of lettuce, a huge slab of red meat oozing blood in its wrapping. Charles had to gulp down the sour fluid rising from his middle.

The women smelled. Sylvia stepped back into him when they raised their arms to unload their cart, and he tripped against the cart behind his, apologizing to the grey little lady who stood stone-faced and gave an abrupt twist of her shoulders.

The women's hands moved quickly, black dirt packed under broken nails, slamming items on the counter, slapping off the children who hovered beside them, muttering in a harsh language Charles and Sylvia could not comprehend. Then the thin one moved the cart to the end of the shoot, tossing the loose purchases back inside. Charles noticed the long scars in her ear lobes, as if someone had seized earrings and ripped them out. When the order was totalled, the thick woman pulled a clatter of euro coins from a cloth bag and dropped them in front of the cashier.

Out in the parking lot, Charles and Sylvia saw the women emptying their cart onto the back floor of an old Renault sedan, the children clinging to the four open doors and rocking the car up and down on squeaking springs. A group of men in plaid shirts and shaggy mustaches stood and watched.

"I don't want to come back here," Sylvia told Charles.

Monsieur nodded vigorously when they reported their experience, poised in the middle of the patio, a coiled hose over one shoulder, about to dash from his workshop to his garden. "Of course, of course," he kept saying. "They're gypsies." He shrugged. "That's the way they are."

Charles watched a small green lizard scurry past Sylvia's shoe, then hop into a crevice of the wall. "But why are they allowed to be here?" she asked.

Monsieur patted the tips of his thin mustache with thumb and forefinger. "They go where they like."

"But where do they stay?"

"Everywhere. Anywhere. In their cars and their trailers. They find an empty field."

"But it's so lovely here." She glanced up at the brilliant sun, the pure blue sky, and contorted her face. "They make it ugly." Charles was disturbed to see her so agitated. He always found her poised and dainty; but lately, remembering how long they had been together, he had the sensation that she was shrinking, withering with the years.

"Do they steal?" Charles asked.

Monsieur pointed to the metal pen with its two large mixed-breed hounds, dogs that barked fiercely whenever Charles and Sylvia drove up to their wing of the farmhouse. "People who live in the country let their dogs loose in the darkness." His property was several miles away from the town, at the end of a long dirt drive, isolated on the bank of a canal. "But the stealing may only be gossip?"

"Have any gypsies come here?" Sylvia said.

"Ask the dogs, Madame." Monsieur's mouth hinted at a smile.

Charles and Sylvia took care to secure the shutter hasps and double lock the wooden front door to their apartment whenever they went out. Each time they returned, as their car thumped up the ruts of the dirt drive, Charles imagined discovering the wood splintered, their clothes gone, the rooms stripped bare of Monsieur's furniture, even the gas stove torn from the wall.

But he said nothing to Sylvia even though he suspected an identical apprehension behind her troubled eyes.

They avoided the Intermarché, paying more at the shops in the village, using the large market only during the midday hours when the other stores were closed and they had no choice. But first they would scan the parking lot for the gypsies, almost always finding the old Renault with paint so worn patches of bare metal glinted under the sun. And a dented white van beside it, with shreds of colored cloth hanging over the slits of windows, the men leaning against the sides, sucking stubs of cigarettes in cupped hands, the children running shoeless across the blacktop, darting in and out of the moving cars, the mothers cursing and swatting at them whenever they dashed by. Charles would leave Sylvia in the car while he did the shopping, avoiding the gypsies in a wide circle, she rolling up windows and locking doors no matter how hot the day.

He would try all the locks before he stepped away.

At night when the lights were out and the bedroom in total darkness, they would lay in the sealed apartment on guard for odd sounds, neither admitting sleeplessness, even though each knew the other could feel it. Nights when Monsieur pumped water from the canal to his garden, they listened to the constant throb of the motor on the bank and the slow trickling into the roots of the plants. They could hear insects and, occasionally, a lizard rushing through leaves. Then one of the dogs would bark, a sharp report that made them shudder against the mattress as if in a spasm. Sometimes Sylvia would sit bolt upright and Charles would clutch the pillow.

Once he whispered, "It's all right. The dogs are fierce. Monsieur has guns." But he could feel her shaking her head in the pitch black. "I don't know. I can't be sure."

Crossing the parking lot at the Intermarché with two baguettes under his arm, Charles saw their car surrounded by gypsy children silently peering in the windows at Sylvia, and he tried to run despite his age and the stiffness in his legs. "Get away!" he called, "Get away!" even though he was passing close to the car and the van, to the men and women who stopped their conversations to stare at him as he bore down on their children.

The children did not move, even when he stood above them and shouted, gazing up blankly as if they did not understand his concern. As he raised a baguette over his head like a club, they scampered off without a sound, not the scornful laughter he expected.

When he unlocked the car, Sylvia was huddled in her seat, sobbing. "Now they know who we are, and they'll never forget."

He saw the children's hand prints smeared across every window.

In the evenings Sylvia would not even leave the room to stroll the path from the patio to the canal. She would rush from the car to the apartment and bolt the door, never cracking the shutters now, not even when Monsieur and Madame in the rooms above them opened wide for the cooling crossbreezes at the end of day.

"My wife has great fear," Charles told Monsieur. "The gypsies."

Monsieur stoked his chin. "They are only people who live in their own way."

"It's not a good way."

"Who are we to say?" Monsieur spread his hands apart, palms upward, and looked to the sky.

They kept lights on through the night, bulbs glaring in every room. Exhausted, they napped on and off in the heat of the day though the sealed apartment was stifling. They rarely left the grounds now except for quick morning runs into the town as soon as the shops opened. Early as it was, they were sure they noted the gypsy car on one street, the van on another, Charles glancing in the mirror to see if they were being followed.

In the heat of the day, their car coated with dust at the end of the drive, they sat in the shade of the patio to watch the lizards skitter across the stones. The dogs knew Charles and Sylvia and rarely barked at their movements, only if someone passed close to their cage. Then they would go wild with ear-splitting yelps that made them both cringe.

Madame did laundry in the mornings and spent the rest of the day with one of her daughters. Monsieur, retired from his business, rushed from garden to workshop, constantly back and forth with intense movements. Now and then, he would pause for a moment to exchange a sentence or two, never once asking why they went nowhere when there was so much beauty all around them—villages growing from the mountainsides, fields red with poppies, purple with lavender, the rivers, the sea, mountains sparking with silver, the brilliance of the light.

A lizard posed rigid on a rock, absorbing the sun. Charles saw Sylvia's hands clench the arms of her chair as she gazed beyond the dirt drive toward the distant hills.

While he was thinking of something to say, her eyes filled with tears. "Why can't other people be like us?" she asked.

"How's that?"

"Innocent."

CIGARETTES

Humiliated to be denied matches, to have to beg for a light, Jane smoked constantly, starting the next cigarette from the glow of the last, fumbling with nicotine-yellow fingers. The others watched hungrily each time she lit, just as she watched them. They knew each other through their cigarettes.

Most of the day Shirelle plowed up and down the corridor with a furious stomp, her great buttocks pumping under yellow stretch pants. But when she wanted a cigarette she shuffled, rubbed her clumsy knuckles into the cropped stubs of her hair, cast eyes down at her shoetips, called Jane "Miss" as if forgetting how she slapped at Jane's breasts in the shower. "Please. Miss, can I have one of them cigarettes? Oh please, Miss."

Lila wore glasses so thick her eyes seemed liquid behind them, clown circles of orange rouge smeared on her cheeks, bright orange lipstick across her flabby mouth. She would clutch at an arm and plead hoarsely, "Just one cigarette, honey. I'm dying for a cigarette. Just one and I'll go away. You don't know how bad it is, honey." Lila clung with an iron grip, chanting her endless pleas. The others had to pry at her fingers.

Old Aunt Minnie, scrawny, toothless, hunched like a sickle, never asked, never spoke to a living soul, but spent every waking hour in an obsessive search for butts, picking through the ash trays, dumping the wastebaskets on the floor and sorting through crumpled litter. Outside, she would drop to her knees, sweeping the sidewalks with her fingertips. She crept under bushes, peered into gutters, any place there might be a butt, stuffing her findings into the two patch pockets of her perpetual housedress, storing her hoard in a secret place no one was ever able to find, not even

Gladys on the night she tore apart Aunt Minnie's bed in a nicotine fit.

Once, when the two of them were apart from the others, Aunt Minnie tapped Jane on the shoulder and slowly opened her fist to display a cluster of butts. Jane tried to give her a whole new cigarette, but the old lady shook her head frantically and hurried away. People never saw Aunt Minnie smoke.

Shirelle even begged from Aunt Minnie though Aunt Minnie didn't seem to hear a word she said. Gladys, tall, narrow-hipped, broad-shouldered, would field strip her butts in front of the old lady, holding them inches from her dull eyes, slitting the paper with a honed fingernail, separating the strands of tobacco in a palm, blowing them in her face with a whoosh of breath.

Annie did everything for God. She jumped for God, each night for an hour, hopping from mattress to floor and back again, flopping loose, naked flesh, shrilling at the top of her voice. "I'm jumping for God! God wants me to jump! God wants me to smoke! God commands that you give me a cigarette!"

Bettylou, the youngest of them all, a pretty girl if it hadn't been for festering acne and the wandering roll of her eyes, collapsed on the floor with an infant wail when denied a cigarette, until—exhausted— she rolled on her side, curled knees into her chest, and stuck her thumb in her mouth.

Marcy was a lady. She had more cigarettes than any of the others, often a carton at a time, gave freely but with carefully defined limits. The records in her head were so accurate no one argued. "No more, Shirelle. You've already had two today." She always spoke sweetly. Everyone, even Lila, kept a distance when she pressed her face against the wall and trembled with a quiet weeping.

Marcy would let Jane borrow whole packs, knowing that Jane would repay. And Jane forced herself never to forget those debts, lay awake repeating each one over and over until it was beaten into her memory.

With everyone watching, just as Shirelle was about to take a light from Marcy, Gladys, face frozen in a scowl, came up from behind and slapped the back of her head, jarring the fresh cigarette from her lips.

It rolled across the tiles until Gladys stopped it with a foot. She wore no shoes, only knee socks bulging with tucked-in jeans. "Please, Miss Gladys," Shirelle moaned, "give it back. I need it awful." Gladys ground the paper under her toes, kicked the filter against the baseboard, then assumed a cock-fisted pose. Shirelle hurled her bulk into her before Gladys could throw a punch. "Motherfucking bitch!" Shirelle jabbed and bit. Gladys attacked with knees and elbows, hard tight jabs with her knuckles. Jane and Marcy scurried away, Lila clutched her own wrist and stood rigid, Aunt Minnie huddled into a comer, Annie bounced on her mattress and shrieked for God, Bettylou emitted an unending wail. Shirts ripped, Shirelle's mouth gushing blood, Gladys's back slashed with deep gouges, the two tumbled to the tiles in a twisted embrace.

Gladys usually ignored Jane, but the next evening, out at the vending machines, she seized Jane's hand just as she reached into the bin for a new pack. "Those are mine," Gladys told her. Before Jane could protest, Gladys hit her twice, a slap across the mouth, knuckles hard into her eye socket. Jane saw a purple swirl and felt her knees give way.

She found herself on her bed in darkness, shoes still on, the pack clenched in her fist. Her stomach throbbed, her face screamed pain. She pulled herself up and out into the corridor, inching against the wall until she pushed through a door and stood before a lighted mirror. Her cheeks and temple were bloated with yellow bruises, her left eye a throbbing slit. She retched into the sink and then washed the pack, wiping it dry against her gown, again and again. Slowly she removed the cellophane, tore open a corner of the foil, and slid a filter between her swollen lips. Aching, brain on fire, she crept along the corridor in search of a match, the eyes of the others burning through the night.

TOBAR'S JOURNEY

Though it was a crystal clear day, the air weightless, the sky brilliant blue, Tobar felt submerged, every movement a struggle against an opaque current.

He groped his fingers across his eyes to pull away the film that fogged his vision. He had been feverish when he began his journey, stumbling through the maze of streets around the central terminal as if his body were about to burst into flames; but now, as he slumped on a bench in front of a strange provincial station, his flesh congealed like cold clay.

Tobar pressed his head against the rough stone of the building and gasped for air. When he reached down to touch his suitcase, he realized he had left it in the coach. The train stood waiting on the track across the platform, but he did not think to retrieve it, even though he had packed the suitcase with fierce urgency. He sat immobile when the train began to move and looked up only when it disappeared into the hills beyond the town.

A tall matron, severely dressed in a green wool suit, took a place on the bench beside him, her matched cases strapped to a wheeled cart. Tobar remembered he was supposed to change trains at this station.

"Where do I go next?" he asked the woman, but heard his words as babbling. She looked at him with distaste yet did not move away from him. It struck him that he had not used her language and he made himself speak again.

"Ich verstehe sie nicht," she said, pulling the luggage closer to her.

Then he recalled his destination and named a village high in the mountains, a place he had chosen at the central terminal, lurching forward and pressing a finger down onto a wall map.

"Ja." The woman nodded, releasing the handle of her cart, and gestured toward a narrow track set into the cobblestone square across from the station.

Tobar closed his eyes, and when he opened them again, an engine and two red cars waited on the track, one carrying a large round container and the other for passengers. He turned to the woman to ask where they had come from, but she was gone.

Before he could make himself move, he had to imagine himself rising from the bench, standing unsteadily, and crossing the cobblestones to the passenger car. Then he was able to flatten his palms on the bench slats to push upward, willing each leg forward one at a time until he stood by the steps of the red car and gripped the railing.

The conductor asked for his ticket, a lean man in a blue uniform with a stiff peaked cap, his face thin and deeply creased, eyeglasses framed with wire so narrow the lenses seemed to float above his face.

When Tobar boarded the car, a few people already were scattered among the wooden bench seats. A plump man in a zippered jacket watched him with a sidelong glance, leaning his elbows out a opened window and whistling a tune Tobar did not recognize. A habited nun followed his movements from behind dark glasses. An elderly woman with tightly curled white hair and large chin moles scrutinized him openly. The only people seated together were three hikers whose backpacks lay in the overhead racks, two deeply tanned men and a plain woman with long muscled legs in shorts and climbing boots.

Stepping like an intruder, Tobar took a seat in the left row several benches behind the nun. Then he noticed that a windowed metal partition divided the car. In the other half, alone in a seat against the front wall, facing the others, sat a short round old man totally bald except for bristle at his temples. He wore heavy grey trousers pulled up to his chest with leather suspenders and a sleeveless undershirt. Streams of smoke emerged from a thick cigar gripped between his teeth.

The people looked at their watches, the nun's delicate gold, the climbers' black-banded sport chronometers, the whistler's jeweled and glittering. The grey-haired woman kept hers hidden under the raised cuff of her jacket. When the conductor waved a brass lantern and stepped aboard, Tobar felt the car wrench forward.

A woman's voice called out, frantic for the train to wait. But the conductor made no move to help her even though he stood an arm's length from the door. A young woman yanked at the handle and lunged into the aisle. She was holding a small boy, little more than a baby, who struggled against her, kicking and shrieking.

Tobar realized that he was the only one who turned in his seat to witness their entrance. The old man with the cigar, already riding backwards, followed their movements with a blank look. But Tobar sensed that for an instant the man's eyes met the young woman's.

He was suddenly seeing everything in this car with a startling lucidity, as if he viewed the scene through a perfectly polished lens.

The young woman carried the squirming boy to a bench across from his. He observed them closely without appearing to be watching. She was young and very beautiful, her glistening dark hair cut short, her face finely boned, her skin golden. He could not make himself stop looking, certain that he would always remember her as though she were in the same room with him.

The boy was kicking his feet, flailing arms, screaming, "Papa, Papa," but the young woman just held him firm on her lap and whispered, "Shhh." She sat serene, eyelids dropped, lips turned at the edge of a smile.

Tobar was struck by the pale blondness of the boy, while the young woman was so dark. But the child was beautiful too, even with his face knotted in tantrum.

The train left the town behind and followed the curve of a rushing river, a glimmering white surface channeled between high stone banks. At times the turns were so sharp Tobar could see the large container on the car behind.

The young woman gestured to the white-haired woman and, even though Tobar did not see a response, moved to the bench beside her. The boy was still screaming, "Papa, Papa." But for Tobar the sound merged with the churning of the train. The older woman stood to reach out and take the boy into her arms, cradling him against her breast and crooning softly. The boy quieted, blue eyes gazing fascinated at the woman's moles, although he did not reach to touch them.

The young woman stood and slid out to the aisle, walking back and forth from the conductor's seat to the partition for the smoking section. Despite the swaying of the train she did not lose her balance. She wore white slacks and a striped jersey that emphasized her breasts. Tobar realized that she carried no purse, that she had boarded the train without one, only the struggling child in her arms. The boy began bawling again, but she ignored him until she had made several more passes up and down the car. Then, without a word, she lifted him from the grey-haired woman and returned to her seat.

The old man with the cigar, alone in the smoking section, was staring up at the steel ceiling. Tobar, following his gaze, saw nothing but the welded seams of enameled metal. As the train accelerated, the man's smoke drifted in through the open window by the whistler. The heavy odor turned Tobar's stomach; he imagined ripping the cigar from the man's mouth and crushing it under his shoe. Anger tore at his ribcage like claws slashing his flesh. He cried out, then wasn't sure he had made the sound aloud.

When he looked around the car, no one appeared to have heard. The child whimpered now; the plump man still whistled. Everyone else sat in silence. Something about the grey-haired woman struck him. When she had stood to take the child, her legs had been unnaturally short; seated, her torso had made her seem of normal height. The cigar smoker's legs were also very short, protruding thickly from his round center, not even reaching the floor. Perhaps he and the woman were a couple, seated apart because of his smoking, ignoring each other like people who had hated through fifty years of marriage.

Tobar closed his eyes at a wave of nausea. His flesh trembled with chill; beads of cold sweat ran down his face. He tried to look out the window.

The train was climbing now. Tobar could feel its strain wrenching through his own body, rising and turning, twisting up into the mountains. The track clung to an edge of rock, poised above deep valleys, tall thin pines trees above and below, looming canopies of dark green ahead in the train's path. A river twined through a rock-strewn bed two hundred feet below. When the train hung above it suspended on a narrow bridge of iron girders, Tobar sensed that all he had to do was heave against the side of the coach to make them all plunge into the abyss. He squeezed his eyes and gripped the bench.

He opened them again when the train slowed and saw a crew of workmen in orange coveralls digging at the stones alongside the track. As the train crawled past, they tapped on the windows with the handles of their shovels. One worker, young and handsome, his hair neatly parted, walked alongside the car directly beside the seat with the young woman and child. He stared at her without a greeting. Tobar couldn't see if she was staring back. None of the passengers were responding to the workmen. The boy buried his face against the seatback and began screaming again.

Soon after they left the workmen behind, the train came to a stop beside a small building of varnished wood. A station sign hung above a red-painted door. Tobar saw no houses, no evidence of habitation to justify a stop, only three curtained windows above flower boxes on the second story of the station. It's very beautiful here, in these mountains, Tobar thought, but the recognition gave him no joy.

The train waited at this stop although nothing seemed to be happening. The car vibrated with the idling of the engine. Each minute of the waiting was excruciating to Tobar. The others seemed very patient, as if they had made this trip a hundred times and knew everything that would happen next. But he felt trapped by the stillness, desperate to reach a destination.

When the conductor called out and waved to the engineer, the old man with the cigar suddenly stood, rushed to the car door, and jumped to the ground. Tobar had the sensation that the man was abandoning his wife. He expected her to cry his name as if the man had hurt her deeply. But she did not make a sound. When the train rounded a bend a hundred yards ahead, the man was still standing by the edge of the track watching something beyond the engine.

The young woman hoisted the boy over her shoulder and slid to the aisle seat of the bench. The boy's face was only a few feet away from Tobar now. At first he stared at Tobar with unblinking bewildered eyes. Then his mouth began to tremble. Please don't cry, Tobar begged silently.

But before there was a sound, the woman rose and quickly carried the boy through the door into the empty smoking section. She sat with her back against the metal partition. Tobar could see her dark hair through the glass window but not the boy on her lap. He found himself wanting to move into the seat beside her, as if the partition would shut them away from all the others, as if they would be sealed in a private world. You are very beautiful, he would tell her, so very beautiful. Then he would reach out a hand to touch her face. He imagined her pressing her cheek against his palm. If she would only show him kindness, the pain behind his eyes would disappear, the anguish in his heart.

The train climbed higher. A waterfall sprayed like white steam from the mountainside into the valley below. The distant peaks were capped with ice, etched against the rich blue of the sky. I am surrounded by beauty, Tobar thought, and wished he could weep. A room in the city burned into his vision, the walls swallowed in grey, a child sprawled and staring upward with huge fixed eyes, a woman's mouth grotesque in screams that drove knives through his skull, a scene of absolute ugliness.

Tobar shook his head to force the screams away, as if the others could hear everything. But they appeared to ignore him even though he was certain they could read his soul.

The hikers spread out a large map full across their laps, one of the men pointing to a spot on the paper and then outside the window. The whistler removed a half-eaten sandwich from a small canvas bag on his lap. He reached across the aisle to offer it to the nun in dark glasses. She shook her head, and the man took a large bite, crunching the hard crust and spraying crumbs from his lips. Even though the man was not whistling now, Tobar kept hearing the tune.

The train was crawling again, the car's wheels grinding against hard steel. Another group of workmen in orange backed off the track to let it pass. Not one of them waved. Their stolid faces peered into the car. Tobar was startled to see the same neatly combed man they had passed down the mountainside fifteen minutes before. The man met

Tobar's eyes with a look of fury. Tobar sensed that if the man had held a gun at that instant he would be dead.

The man gestured and ran ahead, faster than the train, until he was even with the woman and child. Through the partition Tobar could see the man's mouth moving urgently as she leaned toward the window. Then the man turned away and disappeared into the shadows of the trees.

Tobar sensed great threat. He told himself he should go to the young woman and warn her. But he sat frozen while the train crested on the mountain and shook with a downhill surge.

The young woman pushed through the door from the smoking section back into the compartment with the other passengers. When the train lurched, she grasped the seatback in front of Tobar for balance. She glanced down at him. Her beauty made him gasp. He reached out to cover her hand with his, to ask for forgiveness, but she was already sitting in her old seat.

When it struck him that she was alone, Tobar wondered why she had left the boy behind in the smoking compartment. Perhaps he had finally fallen asleep, stretched out full-length on the bench. Yet she didn't have to move so far away. There were empty seats all around the child.

The train stopped again at a station, this time at a cluster of homes built onto the mountainside. A couple boarded, a man and a woman, both thick and sinewy, in the midst of an animated conversation. The conductor walked through the car with them, talking just as excitedly. The three of them sat together in the smoking section and lit cigarettes, waving them from their fingertips with emphatic hand gestures. The boy was alone with them in a smoke-filled compartment, and still the young woman ignored him.

Tobar made himself stand. The others were watching him; the hikers put down their map; the whistler's tune became inaudible. Tobar's face burned with shame; sweat ran down his chest. He stepped back to the smoking compartment but did not enter. He paused at the door and looked down to the seat where he expected to see the boy. The bench was empty.

He pushed through the door and searched the other seats, knelt down to see the floor beneath them. There was no boy. Tobar shook the sleeve of the conductor's blue uniform. "The child! The child!" he said in his own language. The couple stopped their conversation; the seated conductor glared at the hand on his arm. Tobar drew away as if it had been stung. "Das kind," he remembered to say and pointed at the empty bench. The couple gave the conductor a puzzled look. He shrugged, turned his back to Tobar, and revived their discussion.

Tobar bolted toward the other compartment, stumbling as his shoulder hit the partition door, and fell on his hands and knees. No one moved to help him.

Too shaken to stand, he crawled back to where the young woman sat, his eyes at a level with her knees, and groped in his memory for the simplest vocabulary. "Wo ist das kind?" he asked tentatively, and then loudly, "Wo ist das kind?"

She gazed down at him with serene calm.

Tobar shuddered, suddenly tasting a sour dread. He pulled himself up and turned to the others in the car, appealing to them with a gesture. They returned empty gazes.

He chose the nun and sat next to her, speaking frantically and pointing back at the young woman. "Das kind! Das kind ist gegangen!"

She took his hand in both of hers and patted it soothingly. "So, so," she crooned.

He pulled away and turned toward the whistling man, then the old woman and the hikers. All shrank back even before he took a step, alarm on their faces. The old woman held her arms in front of her face as if terrified. The young woman shook her head and parted her lips as if to speak, exposing her perfect teeth.

Then Tobar understood what had happened. She had passed the child to the workman; he was her lover; they had stolen someone's child.

Tobar stood among them ready to reveal what he knew had happened. He would express himself calmly so there would be no misunderstanding. But when he opened his mouth, his tongue bloated against his palate. He was choking on his own words.

Tobar shuddered and sank onto a bench. Tears welled in his eyes, ran down onto his cheeks, and in seconds his body heaved with sobbing. When he finished, his throat burned. The others were silent, looking down at the floor, out the window, deliberately avoiding his presence.

Tobar spread his hands on his thighs, let his arms fall limp, and forced his breathing to be steady. For the rest of his journey he watched only the scabs on his knuckles, his cracked and crusted fingernails. He knew the train had reached its final stop high in the mountains when the other passengers stirred, the hikers reaching up for their packs, clanking buckles as they strapped them on their backs. Tobar sat while they filed past him toward the door without a glance in his direction.

When the car was empty, he moved to get off. The conductor was waiting at the foot of the two metal steps, his thin face grave, the sunlight gleaming from his lenses. Tobar expected the man to block his way and trap him on the train. But he only grunted something Tobar could not understand.

Even though the sun was strong, the cold mountain air stung his lungs. Tobar saw that he wore only a shirt. He was sure he had begun his journey with a coat, though he could not remember the color or the material.

The station was a small stone building across a street from a small lake. Beyond, on all sides of the town, rose the peaks of mountains, brown snow-patched rock far above the tree line. On the other side of the tracks, away from the station and the village, the hillside dropped off quickly, thickly wooded as far as Tobar could see. The sun reflecting off the deep green of the trees made his eyes ache.

The whistler was helping the nun into a taxi, his suitcase beside hers in the open trunk. The hikers, barelegged, pack tops high above their heads, were striding toward an inn, the talking couple close behind them. The grey-haired woman was already gone. Only the young woman remained at the station, stepping impatiently back and forth between two stone pillars. Tobar was drawn to her but knew he should not approach yet. He would watch and wait, icy calm under the dazzling sun.

His stillness astonished him. He had the sensation that his own life was finally vanishing, that he had disappeared behind an invisible barrier and rematerialized here, in this place, as part of another existence.

A large black car drove up the street from around the pond. It stopped directly in front of the young woman. A man with a beard and a woman in a fur wrap stepped out, both elegantly dressed. In turn they held the young woman's shoulders and touched their cheeks to hers. She clutched at their clothing with agitated gestures and spoke frantically. The woman pointed to the back seat of the car.

The man opened the door and stooped to reach inside. He lifted out a small boy who was yawning and stretching, just awakened from a nap, the same age as the child on the train, but dark-haired and dark-eyed like the young woman. The man passed the boy to her, and she seized him in her arms, eagerly kissing his face, his ears, the top of his head.

Tobar edged closer to the group, stepping carefully so that no one would notice. When he realized what he must do, a shock racked his body, as if a taut wire had snapped in the center of his being. He broke into a run, his brain jarred each time his heels pounded the earth. With a thrust of his shoulder he forced the bearded man aside and wrenched the boy from the young woman's embrace.

Tobar heard her shrieks behind him as he leaped across the track and plunged down into the trees on the hillside. Another woman screaming. Another child. He tripped on a root and tumbled headfirst, wrapping his body around the boy. He let himself roll through a clearing, quickly stood with one motion, and sensed himself being swallowed by the chill, dark shade.

The boy was wailing, clawing at his face. Branches slashed his flesh. Tobar tasted blood, felt it flowing into his eyes. Now, blinded, here in this strange woods, he was certain the workman in orange was rushing toward him with the other boy, maddened with hatred.

His clothes torn, his lungs aching, his heart seared, he longed for their meeting. The boy dug his teeth into Tobar's jaw, kicked his stomach, flailed shoes at his groin. Tobar screamed and hurled into the darkness.

GOGGLES

When he looked in the mirror, Weigand saw a pair of grey leather goggles strapped around his face, convex in shape, tapering up to two tiny openings. The mirror seemed fogged, and what he saw was blurred.

He pushed his face to the mirror and peered at the reflection, as if looking closely would explain what had happened to his own glasses, the ones he had worn as long as he could remember, thick lenses in heavy plastic frames.

Weigand had never seen these goggles before or anything like them. He touched the leather with his fingertip and found it oily, then brought the finger to his nose, recoiling from the foul smell. It was like wearing a dead animal on his skin.

Weigand recalled an optical device his doctor had worn when examining him, but that was black metal and apparently magnified, the doctor studying him up and down, from his ears to the veins on his feet, making odd grunting noises as if he were finding things he shouldn't. "What is it?" Weigand had asked, his blood suddenly chill. "What's wrong?" "Nothing," the doctor had told him, and continued observing and grunting. As Weigand dressed, he said he would send a report, but never did.

These goggles did not magnify. They had no lenses. They barely allowed light to enter through the two small holes. His range of vision was constricted to a circle directly in front of him. When he tried to unbuckle the strap at the back of his head, he found the leather rigid and unyielding. And he could not slide it upward. The strap was very tight, as if glued to his flesh.

Weigand realized that his face was not being reflected in a real mirror, but in a fragment of glass hung on a dark wall. He turned to see the room he was in and found that he could barely move his body. The walls were close on every side, raw wood rough to the touch, painted a dull black. He rubbed then with his fingertip, expecting the paint to smear and, instead, imbedded a splinter deep in his flesh. With a wince, he pulled it loose with his teeth and sucked at the wound. There was no blood, not even a tiny bubble.

A dim light glowed in the room, but Weigand could not find its source. Other than the piece of glass, the space was empty. He reached out again, probing the corners and felt a small metal hinge, another several feet below it. This must be the door, though he saw no handle. He pushed with his hand, then with both hands. The wood held firm. Now he braced himself and kicked out, hard. The door parted, just a crack. A sudden brightness rushed in, and he had to close his eyes, slap his hand over the goggles.

When he could look out, he saw a large illuminated space with pure white walls. People stood in small groups, drinks in one hand and plates in the other, talking eagerly, smiling, clearly happy to be with each other. Weigand had to move his head up and down, from side to side, to take them all in through the small circles of his vision.

He forced at the door with all his weight, again and again, feeling it scrape against a rough surface, then allow enough space for him to wedge himself into the room. No one noticed his entrance. He looked back into the tiny room and quickly closed the door to hide the black interior. In all this whiteness, he felt shame.

A waiter in a linen jacket stopped near Weigand, back to him, as he offered a silver tray of food to three people only a few feet away. Weigand realized that he was terribly hungry, as if he had not eaten in days. When he tried to reach around the waiter, the man stepped away. Though Weigand tried to follow, his path was blocked. "Please," he said, but the people would not move.

Directly in front of him, a couple was dancing, the man in a white suit, the woman in silk, her skirt swirling around taut calves. For the first time, Weigand heard music, low throbbing strings, almost a drone, totally unlike the quick rhythmic steps of the dancers. No one else was dancing.

The woman suddenly stopped and stared directly at him, her tight pinched face set in an angry expression. He expected her to curse his watching, and he was about to explain that he had done nothing wrong. Then the man turned face forward, an arm around the woman's waist. It was Weigand's doctor, much taller than he remembered him, elegant.

"Why are you here?" Weigand asked.

"Why am I here?" The doctor raised an eyebrow, and the woman laughed.

Weigand cupped his hands over the goggles. "Why am I wearing these?"

"I prescribed them."

"For what?"

The doctor stiffened. "I'm a physician. I know what I'm doing."

"Where are my glasses?"

This time the doctor gave a slight curl to his lips, almost a smile. "Lila has them."

The woman unsnapped a small pouch fixed to her wrist with a fine golden chain and drew out Weigand's glasses. When he reached for them, she retreated with three quick dance steps, clicking her high heels on the marble floor. She held the glasses over her head. This time he lunged, but the doctor blocked his way, roughly, giving him pain.

"Why can't I have my glasses?" he pleaded.

The woman and the doctor looked at each other. She spoke. "You don't need them now."

"Why?"

After what seemed like a very long silence, the doctor reached up and pinched the goggles shut, first the left and then the right. Weigand could see only darkness. He felt a force at his back, pushing him forward, sensed people parting to make a path for him. At the end, he stumbled over a threshold, thrusting out his hands and scraping rough wood. The door closed with a cry like the shriek of an animal.

VÉRITÉ

Andrew overslept. Usually he was up at 5 but must have dozed after slapping off the alarm, until a squeal of brakes and a metallic rattle made him sit bolt upright and throw off the covers at 5:15. Some vehicle was out in the road, much louder than the Audis and Infinitis of his condominium neighbors. He peeked through the vertical blinds and saw a van at the curb, unmarked, polished grey paint gleaming through the haze of early morning, what looked like a miniature radar antenna turning slowly on the roof.

The timed coffee maker in the kitchenette gave a long gurgle that signaled the end of brewing. Andrew was in and out of the shower in three minutes, then decided to duck onto the driveway for the newspaper, wrapped in a large white bath towel from armpits to ankles.

Just as he scooped up the paper and turned back toward the open door, he heard a voice. "That's terrific, Andrew. It will make a great beginning. I like the towel effect."

A man in a navy turtleneck and tie-died jeans stepped out of the van carrying a leather briefcase. He was tall, thin, and completely bald, though he didn't look more than 30.

"What's going on?" Andrew said, tucking the towel more firmly and glancing down at his bare feet.

"We're the video crew. I'm Jeb." He reached out a hand, but Andrew would not release the towel to shake it. "Molly and Tim are in the van with the gear."

"Crew for what?"

"Your life, of course."

"My life?"

"We have all the signed releases." Jeb unsnapped one catch of his briefcase, then looked at Andrew. "Maybe we should go indoors. You'll be more comfortable there."

"What releases?"

"It's all perfectly legal." Jeb led the way to the door, and when Andrew followed, gestured at the van. The side slid back, and a man and woman, stepped down, both focusing cameras at Andrew. "They'll be using minicams, as you can see. Quite unobtrusive. You'll forget they're there in no time. Molly and Tim are professionals. So am I."

Andrew followed Tim into his own living room, saving his protests until they were inside, out of sight of the neighbors, especially Suzanne in number 143, the blonde with the Lexus, the legs, and the lawn chair, as he always thought of her.

Jeb sat on the sofa, the briefcase now open wide, papers spread on the cushions. Andrew stood beside his entertainment unit trying to devise a strategy, feeling totally vulnerable with only a towel on. Molly and Tim lingered in the front alcove, lenses to their eyes, their faces obscured by little grey boxes. Andrew could hear a faint whir. "This must be a mistake," he said. "Are you sure you want unit 137?"

"These are the releases, all witnessed and notarized." Jeb flipped the edges of the papers and then picked them up one at a time. "We have your landlord, the condo management office, your boss, your coworkers, your mother."

"My mother? What's she got to do with this?"

"Not much probably. You don't see each other all that often. But we'll work in a phone call or two. She's very proud though."

"Proud of what?"

"That we're doing you. I think my mother would feel the same if it were me. But," he gave a short chuckle, "it can't be me, can it?"

"Do what with me?"

"Record your life. From morning till night, even some shots of you sleeping. But just seconds of those. We're not going to do an Andy Warhol." Jeb chuckled again.

"For what purpose?"

"We're not sure yet. We'll have to see what we get in the can, as they used to say. There's all sorts of possibilities. Feature film, PBS, a network series, DVD sales, even an app for the education market."

"But what am I supposed to do? I'm no actor."

"That's exactly what we don't want. Just be yourself."

"I'm nobody special!" Andrew realized he was shouting and saw Jeb wink at Molly and Tim.

"Now you're what all this is about."

"But my life is dull. It bores me most of the time."

"Suzanne in 143 signed a release too."

"I hardly know the woman."

"We're covering all the eventualities."

"What if I say no? Refuse? Don't want any part of it? I never signed anything."

"Ah, but you didn't have to. All that was decided in advance."

"By who?"

"I wasn't in on that phase. They called me on board to direct the taping. It's too late now for any one of us to change our minds. There's already too much invested."

Andrew glanced toward the bedroom, ready to bolt and slam the door. But Tim had already stationed himself in the hallway.

"Look," Jeb said, "why don't you just decide to be a good sport about it? We'll fade into the woodwork. With the new technology, all we need are these minicams, no special lighting or microphones or anything like that. We'll take care of our own food, and one of us will take turns staying in the guest room. No loud CD players or TV when we're there. We use headphones." He tapped his ear.

"Can I get dressed now?" Andrew said. "In private?"

Jeb looked at Molly and Tim, stroked his chin, pondered. "Well, all right. For today."

_____

Andrew didn't even pour himself a cup of coffee. He dumped the carafe in the sink and rinsed it though he suspected Jeb and Molly and

Tim were coveting the aroma. He wasn't going to fall into that trap. No friendships or even politeness, just bare civility.

"Now what?" he asked Jeb when he knotted his tie and slipped on his suit jacket.

"That's up to you. Do whatever you'd do if we weren't here."

"I drive to work."

"Fine."

They followed in the van, managing to stay directly behind despite the heavy traffic, the frequent merges, and the many twists in his route. When he parked in the company lot, the van pulled up in the next row, Jeb leaning a special permit against the windshield.

By the time Andrew reached his floor in the elevator, Molly was already there, walking backwards and shooting him as he walked along the corridor, Tim filming from behind.

He expected an uproar, coworkers three deep and gawking, Charlie Pine, his supervisor even more hyper than usual. But nothing happened. A few people said, "Hi" or "Good morning" when he passed, the way they always did. And Charlie gave a greeting that was half word and half throat clearing. No one even glanced up at the filmers, as if they were as familiar and anonymous as the mail boy.

When Joe Raymond came into his cubicle, Tim at the entrance framing Joe and him in a two-person shot, Andrew expected a question or at least a comment. But Joe only wanted information about a report. Andrew had to be the one to bring up the subject: "What do you think about all this?" "It's something, isn't it?" Joe said and walked out with the file.

"This is all I do," Andrew told Jeb. "Check my email, run through some numbers on the spreadsheet, make a few calls."

"Don't let us stop you," Jeb said.

———————

He didn't work late on purpose, but it gave Andrew a small satisfaction to keep Jeb and the others past 6 without bothering to explain that he was meeting a deadline. He wanted them to think that his behavior was deliberately provoking.

The sunset glittered off the windshield of the van behind him; Andrew couldn't tell who was driving. For a second he contemplated a high-speed chase, squealing about corners, spinning in U-turns, swerving across fields—just like TV. But his Kia was overdue for its tuneup and probably couldn't take the rpms.

When he pulled into his road at the condominium, he could see Suzanne in white shorts, reclining on the lawn chair spread on her patch of grass. Over the past year, since she had moved in, the days she acknowledged him were about fifty-fifty to the days she didn't. But she sat up and waved at Andrew, holding the smile, he thought, a few seconds too long even though she did not shift her eyes to the van.

Andrew zapped his garage door, timing its raising so that he could drive right in. He expected to find the van pulled up in his driveway; but it parked at the curb and only Tim got out, the camera in his hand and two carry-on bags slung over his shoulder, one canvas, the other black leather.

"Where are the others?" Andrew asked.

"I'm on duty tonight." Tim seemed reluctant to speak, making no eye contact, rummaging in the canvas bag as if he needed something. He was a small man, narrow shouldered and wide in the middle, dressed in grey sweat pants and a beige Hard Rock Cafe–London tee shirt.

"Now what?" Andrew said.

"It's not for me to tell you," Tim muttered.

Andrew had planned to prepare a meal from scratch, using his Cuisinart. But with Tim filming from the archway to the kitchenette, he put everything back in the refrigerator and just microwaved a chicken potpie, reading the ingredients aloud as if to let the world know the chemicals he had to ingest.

When the microwave buzzer sounded, he put the container on a plate and popped open a can of beer, wondering if Tim would ask for anything, even to use the kitchen utensils. But Tim pulled a Big Mac from the canvas bag and stood with the burger in one hand and the camera in the other, matching Andrew chew for chew.

Normally, Andrew watched television while he ate, the news or a Seinfeld rerun. But this night he didn't. After he rinsed the plate and took the beer can out to the recycling container in the garage, he reached for a book, a guide to advanced techniques for the company's spreadsheet. After a few minutes of silent reading, he couldn't stand the sound of Tim's breathing and the faint whir of the minicam. He threw the book on a end table and turned on the TV with the remote, scanning the listings and thinking if his life was going to be a matter of public record that he should choose a documentary on the energy crisis. But he flipped past a basketball game just at the moment of an incredible three-point jump shot and stayed with it.

At the next commercial, suddenly exasperated, Andrew said, "This is it? You're just going to stand there making a video of me watching TV?"

Tim shrugged and kept on filming.

When he was tired, it struck Andrew to press the sleep button on the remote so that the set would turn off automatically after he pretended just to be going to the bathroom. Then he slammed the bedroom door and twisted the lock. "Goodnight," he called to Tim.

"I'll be in the guest room," Tim said, his voice hollow, as if he were pressing his mouth to the outside of the door. "We're bringing our own sheets. It's part of the deal."

———————

In the morning, when Andrew came out of his bedroom all showered and dressed, Jeb and Molly were sitting at his table with Tim, the three of them drinking from large containers of Dunkin' Donuts coffee while his own carafe sat full on the counter. He didn't offer them a greeting.

"You're going to have to give us more access," Jeb said.

"To what?"

"Everything you do."

"You're crazy! Some things are private."

"Not for you."

———————

As Andrew backed out of his driveway, Suzanne's garage door opened and her Lexus appeared. She powered down a window and wiggled fingers at him. He could see her lips moving even though his own windows were closed tight. Good morning, Andrew, she seemed to be saying, lipstick very red, teeth very white.

———————

At work he had a meeting in the conference room, Molly there, squatting in a corner. Andrew pointed at her and asked Charlie Pine, "What if we have to talk about something proprietary?" "That's already been taken care of," Charlie said.

At lunch Andrew sat in the cafeteria with Joe Raymond and some of the others, everyone talking about last night's basketball game. He said nothing, even though he thought they were all dead wrong about the defense, instead watching Tim take over from Molly, the two cameras going simultaneously for a few moments until she backed away and stood in the sandwich line.

Tim did him at his desk that afternoon, and Molly followed him home for the evening. Suzanne was out in what seemed to be shorter shorts from the day before, leaning over the shrubbery and trimming uneven shoots with a manicure scissors. This time he slowed down to return her greeting. "Wonderful weather, isn't it?" she said. "You're doing a great job." He pointed at the shrubs. "I like things to look nice," she said.

Andrew wondered what Suzanne would think about Molly following him into the house, and then took a close look at her, shaped exactly like Tim, wearing identical sweatpants and a Hard Rock Cafe–Firenze tee shirt as if it were their uniform.

It was a Friday night, and he'd usually be doing something, calling a friend or seeking a date to go out to dinner or hear music at a local bar. But now he felt odd about involving anyone else in his life, though he did call his mother because she expected him to phone every week.

"Why didn't you warn me what was happening?" he said.

"I wanted it to be a surprise."

"Let me tell you what they're doing?"

"It's probably not a good idea to talk about it. You shouldn't be self-conscious."

"Then what should we talk about?"

"How's work?"

———————

Andrew fixed a sandwich and sat on the couch looking out the window at the clouds at nightfall. When his living room was dark, he saw the lights go on in Suzanne's unit and wondered if she were home for the evening.

"Why don't you turn that thing off?" he said to Molly. "You can't be seeing anything in here."

"It's ok."

"Let's have a conversation," he said. "How did you become a camera person? Did you go to school for it?"

"I'm not supposed to talk to you."

"Why not?"

"The Heisenberg principle."

"What's that?"

"It's better that you don't know."

He sat in darkness watching to see if Suzanne's car would leave or if a car would come for her. But nothing happened. Once he thought he saw a hand spread her verticals, though it could have been the wind.

———————

Saturday he did laundry and vacuumed, Tim relieving Molly at noon. Every time he looked outside, Suzanne was on her lawn chair, reading a thick book. Midafternoon he decided to call a friend, Jimmy Masters, to see if he was free for a drink that evening. They met in a bar called Ernestine's, where Andrew had a hamburger and Jimmy, having eaten at home, just picked at his French fries. Tim kept appearing at different positions in the room, aiming the camera from the next booth, from the balcony, even from behind the bar.

At first, Andrew wasn't going to bring up the subject, but finally couldn't help saying, "You see that guy?"

"I know all about it. They got me to sign a release."

"Today? After I called?"

"No. A week or two ago."

"Do you want to hear about it?"

Jimmy shook his head. "Let's just be normal."

"All this," Andrew said, "makes me realize how dull my life is. How empty."

Jimmy smiled and punched his arm. "Hey, you're okay. You're no different than anybody else."

When Andrew got home, as soon as he entered the unit, he realized that the doors to the bedroom and bathroom were gone. "Hey! Goddamnit!"

"That Jeb's some producer," Tim said, as if talking to himself.

Andrew pulled the shower curtain around him when he stood at the toilet, and the next morning showered in his jockey shorts, especially with Molly filming. This time her tee shirt was from Reykjavik.

"Have you been to all these places?" he asked her.

The head behind the camera shook no. "We never have the time to go anywhere."

"Have there been others like me?"

She wouldn't answer.

Sunday afternoon, when the mall opened, Andrew went to the electronics outlet where he had gotten his CD and DVD players and bought his own minicam, watching from the corner of his eye to see whether Tim had figured out his strategy.

As soon as he got the camera home and charged the battery, he turned it on Tim, taping Tim taping him, the two of then standing there in the living room, feet planted and shooting away. It's like a duel, Andrew thought; but Tim's expression revealed nothing. Perhaps others had done this too; perhaps Jeb had prepared Tim and Molly for anything.

The next day Andrew took the minicam to work, and people were curious about it, wanting to hold it and point, mugging for each other, crowding into group poses, doing everything they wouldn't in front of Jeb's crew. "Why not?" he asked Joe Raymond when the others went back to their desks. "They're professionals," Joe said. "What they're doing is real."

Andrew used the camera whenever he had a chance, even setting in on his desk to catch his own computer screen and his hands on the keyboard. Then suddenly he would swing it around to Tim or Molly, whichever one was at work.

In the evening he walked the paths of the condominium, Molly close behind with her own camera. When he neared Suzanne's unit, she stood and waved, moving toward him and touching the camera in his hand, her fingers covering his. "Isn't that cute?" she said. "Do you want to try it?" he asked. She aimed it at him, backing up, kneeling, sprawling on her lawn chair for the angle. "You'll have to show me what kind of an artist I am, if I have any talent." "I'm sure you do," he said as the camera slipped from her hand to his. She smiled over his shoulder, and when he turned, he saw that Molly was smiling back.

But at the end of three days, Andrew was bored with filming, constantly looking at a world of color through an eyepiece that turned it into tones of grey. The people in the office got tired of posing, the bit quickly stale, their ingenuity dry.

Jeb appeared after dinner the evening Andrew put the camera in a drawer under his sweaters. "We knew you wouldn't keep it up," Jeb said. "Filming is tedious if you don't have a purpose. Your imagination has to see what you're doing as culminating in a product. You were just fooling around."

"I was trying to turn the tables."

"Now you see what a silly idea that was," Jeb said.

———————

Andrew knew he had to do something. His first idea was to go ask Suzanne out for a date and then return to his unit. But as soon as he tried to imagine the evening, he realized that would be exactly what Jeb hoped for. His favorite fantasy in the months since Suzanne's appearance would be playing into their hands.

But as he was lying in bed on a Thursday, in the moments of half-sleep just before the alarm, a strategy struck him. He leaped up and, when he saw Tim in the doorway, started bouncing up and down on the mattress, shouting at the top of his lungs. He threw off his pajamas and pranced around the room naked, turning somersaults down the hallway into the living room, climbing onto the back of the couch and diving into the carpet. For several minutes he swung an imaginary tennis racket as if an opponent were returning his shots from across the room. Then he urinated in the sink, lathered himself from neck to navel, and shaved the left side of his chest.

When he dressed, he turned a pair of old plaid trousers inside out, buttoned a shirt and pulled it backwards over his head, wrapped a tie around his waist, wore one hiking boot and one bedroom slipper, and crushed a hat crown side down on the top of his head.

He wouldn't walk. He moved with two-legged hops, sidewise scuttling, elbow and knee crawling. For breakfast, he poured a mixture of orange juice and coffee into a cereal bowl and ate it with a wooden mixing spoon.

When Andrew went into the garage, considering how it would be to drive all the way to work in reverse, Jeb was leaning against his car door. He reached out for Tim's minicam, opened it, popped out the cassette, and snapped it in half, pulling out yards of thin brown tape and balling it all into a knot. Then he dropped the cassette into a garbage can.

"We won't use any of that stuff," he told Andrew. "Keep it up as long as you like. We've got infinite patience, and we're still under budget."

The next time Andrew planned carefully. Of course, he couldn't consult books or maps or even write anything down. Everything had to be in his head. But he could glance at pamphlets and manuals in his desk for a few seconds in the midst of his real work. He could stay alert every time he walked down a hallway or went to another floor. He even devised alternate strategies for his first steps, knowing what he would eventually do but unable to predict exactly when he would begin. That would involve a little bit of luck.

The break came sooner than Andrew would have guessed. One afternoon not another person was in the hallway of his normally busy building and an elevator was waiting with an open door. He ambled by as if heading somewhere else, then suddenly turned into the car and shoved Molly backwards when she moved to follow, sprawling her against the opposite wall. He punched the button for Lobby again and again until the doors slid shut while Molly was still groping for her scattered equipment.

Once on the main floor, he bolted out to the street, threading through the lanes of traffic waiting at a stoplight. He stopped running a half-block before the Hertz agency to smooth his hair, straighten his tie, and slip a credit card into his palm.

Because his name was already in the computer, he was in a Ford Focus and out on the highway in under ten minutes. But he didn't head to the local airport, assuming that was where Jeb would go when Molly called. He drove three hours to a town just over the state line, left the car in a parking lot, and took a train to a city with a large airport.

In the plane, he was one of the few people in first class, choosing that luxury for the first time in his life because he knew he would never pay any charges billed to his real name.

The plane was bound for Wichita, a city he knew absolutely nothing about, chosen because it was a place he had flipped past on a sales chart. There he would buy a razor and a toothbrush and a suitcase full of new clothes, then take a cash advance large enough for a used car. He would drive out of the city to the most obscure town he could find, destroy all identification, grow a mustache, and start a new life with a new identity. Perhaps someday, from a place no one could ever trace, he would send his mother a postcard: "Don't worry. It's better this way."

In the Wichita airport, as he moved down the ramp from the gate to the waiting room, two people were waiting with minicams pointed right at him, about the same size and shape as Molly and Tim, but wearing powder blue coveralls, clearly other people.

When he saw them, Andrew sat in the middle of the walkway and wept, gradually crying more loudly until he was bawling like a two-year-old, knowing that people were giving him odd looks, old women pausing in uncertainty, a security guard poised with his hand on his pistol butt.

The camera people already had his return ticket, one at each elbow, guiding him back up the ramp. He kept thinking that he would never ever see the Wichita waiting room.

———————————

Two months later, Andrew found himself in his living room with the TV playing a commercial, Molly and Tim on the sofa, she wearing a cocktail dress and he in a pinstriped suit. Tim sat backwards on a wooden chair, tapping the rungs with a ring and apologizing as he did it. "I always get nervous at this stage."

He had brought several bottles of champagne and a meal of takeout Chinese. Molly and Tim were staring down at Tim's watch, then looking up at the screen and back down to the watch again. "It's almost time," she said.

The door chimes sounded once and a moment later a second time. Andrew refused to move. Tim had to get up to answer. It was Suzanne, lovely in a strapless gown. "Hi!" She pecked Jeb on the cheek. "Hi, yourself," he said. And she giggled. "I can't wait."

Andrew turned to her and nodded. When he glanced at the screen again, his face was staring back at him, a resonant announcer's voice speaking his name. And suddenly there he was wrapped in the towel the way it had been on the very first morning. Jeb was laughing. "Great! Great!" Andrew's vision glazed; he wasn't sure if he was watching scenes on tape or reflections of his imagination. "That's me!" Suzanne squealed.

Andrew had to close his eyes, then feared opening them, afraid the face on the screen would be opening his eyes too, that he would be seeing himself live, exactly as he was at that very instant.

Then when he did make himself look again, Jeb and Suzanne were smiling down at him, Molly and Tim both zeroing in with minicams.

125

OUBLIETTE

Moss met the little woman at the village's waterfall where children swung on a knotted rope lashed to a tree branch—a tiny round woman with a dog just as tiny and round, an ugly flat-faced thing at the end of a long leash. The woman wasn't ugly, just ordinary, though startlingly out of place in high heels and a tight white dress that exaggerated the roundness of her body. Moss wore jeans and an old sweatshirt, the children just shorts and tee shirts. One by one they dropped into the swirling pool at the base of the fall, shrieking as they splashed. Moss and the woman were the only adults at the scene.

When she stepped toward him, he wanted to turn away, take the stone path to the village. Even in his short time there, he realized people were always greeting one another. But Moss only responded with a nod. He lifted his feet to avoid tangling with the leash. The woman pointed toward the young people. "I haven't done that in years."

"I've never done anything like that." Moss pictured her hanging from the rope in that dress and heels, falling in and being swept away, dragging the dog after her.

"But it looks so tempting." Her face was round like the rest of her, a button nose, bleached ringlets swirled around her head, circles of blush on her cheeks.

"Not to me." His response came out harsh, and he knew he shouldn't be too unfriendly, not call attention to himself in this small place. He gestured with his head. "The kids like it."

"Why wouldn't they?" She tugged at the leash, the little dog following her back to the houses, dog and mistress walking with tight, abrupt steps, she inhibited by the narrow sheath of her dress.

———————

Moss had chosen the village from a brochure, intrigued by its remoteness and the photo of two rows of dark stone cottages on both sides of a green expanse empty of people. The village lay several miles off the highway on a single-track road walled by tall hedges. His car doors kept brushing the leafy twigs, but he didn't care how scratched the car got. It was old, and he probably would abandon it. The deeper in he drove, the better Moss liked the sense of being hidden. He would be far from everything he had ever known.

His accommodation was a two-room flat, one of four in a grey granite building set back from the others, twenty yards from the waterfall. For several centuries it had been a mill, powered by the current of the narrow stream. But now the wheel was gone, the structure recently converted to spaces for visitors, the rooms small but very neat and clean. He wouldn't unpack his belongings from the canvas duffle, unwilling to disturb the order. The place he had left in the city was a shambles. His doing.

Another car had been parked next to the space he took when he arrived, and he heard movements on the floor above his. The next morning, thankfully, the car was gone. He was there all alone. Even with the windows closed, the sound of rushing water was loud. Its steadiness calmed him as he read his area guidebook, but he couldn't fall asleep. He couldn't remember the last time he had truly slept.

———————

Even before he had picked this village, Moss had planned to walk, disappear into the countryside. The city was no place for walking, the streets thick with vehicle exhaust, the sidewalks crowded, the building walls oppressive. He had been wise enough to break in his boots and buy cushioned socks. Mornings he would pack lunches from the breads and wedges of cheese he had brought, wrap them in plastic and place them in his rucksack with two bottles of beer and an apple.

A path outside the old mill led past the waterfall and up into the hills. The climb was gentle even though the hilltops rose far above the village. At the lower levels stone walls set up barriers too high for him to climb. He had to twist through wooden stiles meant to pen in the sheep and cattle.

Moss had expected the creatures to scatter when he neared, but they gazed at him with placid faces and empty eyes, the cattle swishing tails. Even though they stood their ground, he shouted at them to keep away, stooping to pick up rocks, closing his fists on the sharp edges. The cattle lowered their heads to chew the grasses, the sheep indifferent as Moss passed. He dropped the rocks and kicked at them with the toe of a boot.

The hills rolled gently, linked by a network of thin paths, clear of growth, as if they were a much-traveled thoroughfare, though Moss —to his relief—met no other walkers. He was the lone human on the landscape.

Once he reached a hilltop, he sat on a rock for a bite of lunch, swigs of beer, and looked out over the miles of landscape below, his village's rooftops directly beneath, a curved road, long lines of stone walls stretching between the other villages, farms here and there, scattered livestock, and in a distant cluster of trees the ruins of a castle. He had read about it in the guidebook. In ancient times men died chained in its dungeon, rotted in oubliettes.

He gazed for a hour with the sensation that he was no more than a pair of viewing eyes, the entire world outside him, hoping to free himself of all that lay within. Thoughts, memories, deeds. But even here that was impossible.

As Moss descended toward the village, the path became very steep, forcing him to run to keep his balance. He stumbled on a muddy patch and came down on his backside. There, not far away, the woman with the little dog was staring at him, wearing a different dress just as tight as the other and the same high heels. She wasn't smiling even though his tumble must have looked ridiculous, a comic flailing. Nor did she show concern, just bewilderment, as if his presence were an aberration.

When Moss pulled himself up, he realized his jaw was aching. He must have jarred it when he hit the ground. Rubbing it, he told the woman. "I don't always do that."

"Do what?"

"Fall down."

"Oh, that's all right."

He had no idea what she meant. That for all she cared he could fall again and again? That falling didn't matter? That it made no difference to her what he did?

"You have mud on your trousers."

"I suppose I do."

The dog sniffed his shoes, a creature practically hairless, with great bulging eyes and a bobbed tail. He wondered why anyone would want a dog like that.

"What's its name?" he asked.

"Pumpkin. Precious Pumpkin. What's yours?"

Moss introduced himself.

"I'm called Nella," she told him.

Though she hadn't inquired, he explained he was only there for just a short time.

"I'm new too," she told him. "But I plan to stay. This is the first time in my life I haven't lived in a city."

"What made you leave?"

"I wanted something else."

"And are you finding it here?" Moss realized he was asking for himself.

"It takes time to make friends."

It does if you dress that way, he almost said but didn't, not to a stranger. Instead he shrugged. "I wouldn't know."

"I expect to be happy here," she told him.

When she turned, the little dog rushed to her feet and stayed very close as she walked off with choppy steps, desperate for happiness. He didn't care.

When his food supply dwindled, Moss took to replenishing bread, milk, and cereal in the cramped village shop, but eating most meals in the village pub just a few doors down. It was an ancient building with a doorway so low he had to stoop to enter. If he raised his arms, he could touch the beamed ceiling. The small tables wobbled, and the bartenders, young men both called John, were constantly propping cardboard coasters under the short legs. Most early evenings Moss was the only one ordering a supper.

Despite their names, the Johns couldn't have been more different. The tall, soft John had lived in the village all his life and barely spoke to Moss, though he chatted about livestock and weather with the men who sat at the bar. The shorter John, wiry, with a taut, tense face, liked to hold forth, standing over Moss every time he brought a plate from the kitchen, telling about all the places in the world he had visited, how much he liked the Algarve in Portugal, how he would be off again to somewhere he hadn't picked yet as soon as he had saved up a bit of money. Occasionally, he would ask Moss about his travels, but whenever Moss named a place he interrupted with tales of another.

Each evening as he ducked through the door Moss wondered which John would be on duty. Their schedules seemed arbitrary, beyond prediction. One night he found Travel John unusually silent behind the bar, just listening to the three men perched on stools in front of him. After several minutes, Moss realized just one of the men was doing all the talking, deeply tanned with a head of blond curls, tattoos on both forearms beneath his rolled sleeves, his face weathered.

The man's voice resonated, too loud for the space, echoing off the low ceiling. Moss realized he was telling a story about how he had crashed his sports car and ended up with his face flat against the windshield. He pressed a hand down on his nose and mouth to demonstrate the distortion. The other men were laughing, John too, as if listening to the man were as interesting as a distant locale.

"The dentist was in love with me," the man was saying. "The challenge of the restoration, all the money he would make. What front teeth I didn't knock out immediately were rattling loose. I lived on a diet of soups. And this stuff." He held out his pint glass to more laughter. "It took months of extractions, measurements, plaster modeling, and temporaries. But now I have a bionic mouth. These teeth"—he pulled back his lips and tapped the two in front—"are top of the line. No enamel for me. I've got titanium teeth. Titanium!" He threw his head back in laughter, and the others were roaring.

Moss didn't like the man. He waved the menu over his head to get John's attention.

———————

Unable to sleep again, Moss found himself pacing the small rooms of the apartment at sunrise and decided to go for another walk. When he stepped outside, the village was absolutely quiet, not even a car moving on the narrow road, just the unending rush of the waterfall. He imagined he could hear all the people breathing in their sleep like a single sigh that rustled the leaves.

But as he began his ascent on a path, he saw Nella and the dog ahead of him, she in the dress she had been wearing the first time he saw her, but with a green shawl wrapped about her shoulders and puffy white walking shoes that seemed much too large for her tiny feet. She wasn't moving, standing still while the dog sniffed at a bush, circled it, and stopped to raise a leg. Moss had the thought that she was waiting for him, though she wasn't looking in his direction.

He came up behind, kicking his boots on the ground to alert her. "Good morning, Nella," he called.

"Oh, hello." She didn't return his smile, and Moss knew he was smiling because she amused him, this foolish woman who wanted happiness.

He reached down to pat the dog's head, ready to draw back, expecting a nip. But the dog buried its face in leaves.

"Would you like to walk with us?" she asked.

He looked down at the tight skirt bottom.

"We won't go far."

Moss nodded. "All right. Thanks." He had nothing else to do.

He took half-steps, slowing to her pace, the dog stretching the long leash as it lingered behind. Nella gestured toward the countryside, the hilltops and the village. "It's beautiful here."

"I suppose it is," Moss said. "Is that why you picked it?"

"One reason. But mainly, I picked it because it's not where I was before."

"What was wrong there?"

"I wasn't happy where I was."

"Could you go back if this doesn't work out?"

She nodded. "But it won't be necessary. I'll be fine here. What about you? Will you go back?"

"That may not be such a good idea."

For the first time she gave him a look of real interest. "No people, no person there for you?"

"No. Not there. Not anywhere. Not for a long time."

She nodded. "Yes. It's that way sometimes."

They came to a rise in the path, the worn dirt just wide enough for one person, and Moss stepped aside to let her go first. Halfway up, she tripped on a rock and lost balance, falling back into his grasp, her head no higher than his chest. He felt the warmth of her, the pressure of her roundness. At once he stiffened his arms and held her away. "Sorry," she said.

"Did you hurt yourself?"

"I should go back now."

She asked him to carry the dog. The creature was almost weightless, the bulging eyes gazing up at Moss, the mouth open, saliva drooling onto Moss's hands. He felt the rough, dry coat, breathed the sour dog odor.

Late that afternoon, at loose ends, unwilling to stay in the pristine flat any longer, Moss walked again, taking long strides as if rushing to reach a destination though he really had nowhere to go, nowhere he wanted to be. The sheep and cattle seemed used to him now, barely turning their heads, poised in their stillness like the boulders scattered across the landscape.

Climbing rise after rise, he found himself out of breath and sat to suck in air. A sudden dizziness struck him, and he had to lie back on the grass with eyes closed. When he looked out again, he saw clouds floating in a blue sky, felt the breeze on his face. He sat up, calm now, and looked out across the hills and valleys, everything green, creatures still within stone walls, roofs and chimneys of clustered habitation. The castle ruin in the distance, stark edges jutting among the trees.

His chest heaved with the sense of a great isolation, tears streaking his cheeks, unable to lift a hand to rub them away. Then he buried his face in his knees and shivered with loneliness. It had been a mistake to come here, as if relocation could change the world that lived in his head, the life he had ruined, the woman and children he would never see again.

———————

Moss was blinded when he stepped into the dim pub from the brilliant glow of the setting sun. As he blinked he could hear a voice greeting him. Soft John. Then a sputtering laugh he knew came from the man he thought of as Titanium Teeth. Now he could see they were the only people there, the man perched on a stool, elbows on the bar, John drying glasses but riveted to the man's grin, as if he were showing off those teeth.

"What'll it be?" Soft John said.

Moss tried to decipher the menu chalked on a slate behind the bar. Though it was too early for dinner, he needed food because he hadn't eaten since breakfast. "I'm thinking," he told John.

Titanium Teeth turned his grin to him. "You have yourself a good long think." He began laughing again, John with him.

Moss clenched a fist in his pocket, knowing that if he hit the man once, he wouldn't be able to stop until he had knocked out all those fancy teeth, pulped the smug face. He hadn't hit anyone in months, and then it had been the wrong person. The worst person in the world to receive his rage.

"I've thought as much as I need to," he said and ordered gammon and a pint, then sat at a wobbling table against a far wall, leaning his head against a dark, ancient beam, trying to blot out the pictures swirling through his mind.

"So he just dropped his bar rag and disappeared without a bye your leave," Titanium Teeth was saying.

John shook his head. "It wasn't exactly like that. He gave notice when he came in the morning, did his job as if it were just another day, totaled up the register, gave me a wave, and out the door."

"Do you know where he went?"

"You never know with him. In a month or two we'll get a postcard from some place in the world I've never heard of." John pointed to a corkboard of pinned cards that Moss had never noticed before.

"Was there a problem? He in some kind of trouble?"

"Naw. His only trouble is in his head. Can't stay in one place. All the times he said to me, 'How can you stand it here?'"

Titanium Teeth laughed again. "How can you? When was the last time you left the village?"

"There's nothing I need out there. I'm content."

"Good for you." The man reached out to pat John's shoulder and gestured back toward Moss. "Some of us are just visitors. Maybe we don't know how much we're missing."

"So when are you leaving this time?"

Titanium Teeth shrugged. "It depends."

Moss heard the door open and in the shaft of light from outside saw Pumpkin straining at his leash. He half rose from his chair, ready to greet Nella and invite her to sit with him, realizing he wanted that. Someone to talk to. She paused in the doorway, blinking to adjust her vision just as he had, but didn't look in his direction. Instead she walked right to the bar next to Titanium Teeth. The man knelt and swept up the dog, set it on the stool to his right, scratching his fingers on the tiny head. "Good boy." The dog licked his hand.

Nella watched closely, wearing yet another tight dress and another pair of heels. Titanium Teeth wrapped an arm around her shoulder and gave her a hug. "A drink for the lady, John." She didn't move closer, but she didn't struggle.

The man began telling a story in a low voice, as if he didn't want Moss to hear. When he tapped a tooth, Moss assumed it was about the accident and his dental miracle. Whatever he was saying, it made John laugh so hard he had to rub tears from his eyes. Nella listened with great attention and then broke into a smile. Moss had never seen her smile before. He felt sure Titanium Teeth made a gesture, back toward him, Nella smiling even more broadly, John laughing louder.

Moss finished his meal and drank his beer very deliberately, hearing the seconds ticking in his skull. He pushed back the chair, stood, and put on his jacket. At the bar, he took out his wallet, reached around Titanium Teeth, and dropped a 20 pound note. Titanium Teeth tapped John's chest. "With a tip like that you could give notice yourself and see the world."

Moss bumped his elbow into the man's shoulder, making him topple a half-filled pint. "Jesus, mate!" Titanium Teeth started to get up but turned away when he saw the look on Moss' face. John, head down, wiped the spilled beer with a rag. The dog was snarling, Nella rigid on her stool.

Outside, away from the pub, Moss ran past the lanes of the village, bumping through stiles, stumbling along the path, tripping over stones. He wasn't wearing boots and could feel jagged edges through the thin soles of his shoes. By the time he climbed a hill, the sun had vanished behind a wall of dark clouds coming in from the west. Even with his jacket zipped, Moss shivered in the chill, raindrops sharp on his face.

Creatures clustered about him—sheep with streaks of colored dye on their wool, cattle with bell collars that clanked as they chewed their cud, oblivious to the rain. Before, he hadn't noticed that they all belonged to someone.

Moss plunged ahead toward the hilltops, off the marked trail. He came up against a rusted wire fence much taller than he was and groped for an opening, desperate to get to the other side, pulling at the wire, trying to rip it free from the posts, his hands bleeding. But he wasn't strong enough. He slumped back against the wire, heavy rain now beating down on him, soaking his clothing, turning the earth to mud.

Far below, in the village, a dim light illuminated the pub sign, promising warmth within. Alone in the downpour, Moss pulled his jacket over his head and sealed himself in darkness.

REMOVAL

When Raymond came home that afternoon and unlocked the double bolts, he had to push with his shoulder to force the door open. Something was blocking it, soft and heavy, that felt wedged against the hinges. "Damn!" He squeezed in between the door edge and the frame, then tripped over one end of a very large plastic bag, thinking that was it, the barrier, as if he had solved a problem. The plastic was thick and translucent, with a long zipper across the top, stuffed with cloth of many blurred colors, perhaps clothing, perhaps sheets and towels, or maybe just rags. He started to call his wife's name, Beatrice, but remembered she had told him she would be out for the day.

Beyond the plastic bag, he saw three grey suitcases, cardboard boxes, an empty bird cage on a stand, a table lamp with a torn shade, an ancient manual typewriter, the underside of a rolled rug, a down comforter balled in a heap—all spread between the door and the steps that led downstairs. He and Beatrice lived in small rooms on two levels, the upper with a metal kitchen unit, a sitting area just big enough for two wicker chairs and a narrow dinette, and their bedroom; downstairs, below street level, they just had space for a TV stand and a work table that took up one entire wall. What was all this new stuff? Raymond wondered. Where would they put it? What was she up to?

Then he heard footsteps from below. "Beatrice?" he said. But there was a man, suddenly appearing on the stairway, smiling, a hand extended, a very thin man in dark trousers and a white dress shirt with sleeves rolled up above the elbows. He wore rimless glasses and had a neat little goatee; but his sparse grey hair was tousled as if he had just come from exercising. Raymond had never seen him before.

But before he could ask, the man pumped his hand and said, "I'm Eugene. Beatrice isn't home."

"I know that," Raymond said, his head cocked, expecting the man to go on. But Eugene only pushed the hair back from his forehead and smiled. "Are you sure you have the right apartment?" Raymond asked him.

Eugene laughed, exposing a mouth of very white teeth. "Beatrice must have explained everything."

Raymond shrugged, wondering if it would be a good idea to let this man know Beatrice had told him nothing. "I'd like to hear it from you," he said and felt clever.

"Well, I'll be 62 next month." It struck Raymond that Eugene's teeth were surprisingly good for a man his age. "And my father loved Mozart. He played the piano, not very well, certainly nowhere near good enough to be a professional. But it was Mozart all the time, day and night. I could close my eyes right now and hear him doing the sonatas. When somebody plays Mozart without going flat, my first reaction is that they've made a mistake." He smiled. "But we never escape the memory of our parents, don't you think?"

Raymond nodded even though his had been dead so long he had to take out photos to remember their faces. "Did your father make a living from music?" he asked.

This time Eugene laughed out loud. "Hardly."

"What did he do then?"

"That's another story." A shadow crossed Eugene's face; but then he smiled again. "Of course, he did leave me the piano, and I keep meaning to take lessons. But you know how it is when you're busy."

Raymond looked back to all the boxes and cases and the plastic bag as if he had overlooked a piano during his initial surprise. He knew he should ask Eugene why all this—this stuff was here, but kept putting if off, not sure how he should react if he did not like the answer. So he said, "How long have you known Beatrice?"

"Not very long."

"Where did you two meet?"

Eugene looked up at the ceiling. "Let me see. It was either in a taxi or an elevator. Or it might have been waiting to be seated in a restaurant. One thing you'll learn about me is that I'm not always clear on the details."

"Are you two lovers?" Raymond asked.

"Lovers!" At first Raymond thought Eugene was shocked by the question, then realized it was bewilderment. "I never thought of being Beatrice's lover. It's not that your wife isn't sufficiently attractive. But when you get to my age sex isn't always the first thing that one thinks about. Though it's an interesting idea. It would help pass the time, especially during the winter months, when it gets dark so early. But I imagine you'd mind. Jealousy, and all that."

"I think I would." Beatrice, as far as Raymond knew, had never had a lover, and so he wasn't sure how he'd react.

"Human life can get very complicated," Eugene said, as if it were the first time that idea had ever occurred to him.

"Is all this yours?" Raymond asked, prodding the side of a suitcase with his toe, wondering how hard he would have to kick to make it topple over.

"I'd hoped to have everything downstairs before you got home. Much of it is. But I've never been very good at estimating how long a task will take. I suppose I'm overly optimistic about most things. Did you know you have twelve steps between levels? I must have been up and down twenty times so far."

"You have more?" Raymond asked, and pointed. "Down there?"

"But it only looks like a lot now. When it's all spread out. Normally, I'm a very compact person. Would you like to see downstairs?"

"Yes, I would," Raymond told him, and looked to the door, hoping Beatrice would appear at that moment, even though he knew it was much too early.

"But you won't find the piano." Eugene laughed as if he had made a joke.

Downstairs, shopping bags from a dozen stores were piled on the worktable, suits and trousers and starched shirts draped on hangers over the bench, the television stand dragged out into the middle of the floor, all the prints off the walls, the carpet pulled up at two edges and folded back, what seemed to be a hundred tiny white boxes strewn across the bare wood.

"Of course," Eugene said, "it won't look this way for long."

"What will it look like?" Raymond asked.

"At this moment, that's a bit of a puzzle. But it will all work out. Most things usually do."

"There's not much room," Raymond said.

"I realize that. I'm not a fool." For the first time since they had met, Eugene sounded a bit testy.

"Do you have an arrangement?" Raymond asked. "With Beatrice, I mean?"

"Well, not exactly. I thought we'd settle that later."

"But she knows about all this . . . all these things?"

"That's something we'll have to find out from her, won't we?"

She won't tell me, Raymond said to himself, struck by the expectation that he would never know.

"I hate to ask," Eugene said, "but you're a much younger man, and I could use some help."

"Of course." Raymond followed him upstairs. Eugene gave the comforter a shove, and it flopped down the steps, slowly, tumbling one by one. He gestured to Raymond that he should grip one end of the rolled rug. Together, hoisting it over the railing, they dropped the rug in the center of the floor, then took turns with the boxes, suitcases, lamp, typewriter, and birdcage. They barely had space to walk in the downstairs room, Raymond banging his shins against suitcases, stumbling over boxes.

Finally, only the plastic bag was left. Raymond knew it would take the two of them to maneuver something so large and shapeless. He knelt to get a grip but could barely budge it, as if a great weight were wrapped beneath all the colored cloth.

"What we'll do," Eugene told him after a long silence of contemplation, "is have you back out into the hallway for leverage."

Together they dragged the bag forward to open the door wide enough for Raymond to step outside and squatted at opposite ends of the bag. "Now!" Eugene shouted. "Lift!"

Raymond couldn't close his fingers on the slippery plastic. Something large seemed to be shifting toward him, something soft and warm and pliant. He cried out and spread his arms to fling himself atop the bag, but a great force heaved against him. He lost balance and fell flat out into the hallway. The door slammed shut in front of him.

He stayed calm, reaching into his pocket for keys, carefully selecting those for the double bolts, inserting and turning the bottom one until the bolt slid back. But as hard as he pushed the top key wouldn't go in. He tried all the other keys one at a time, rattled the knob. Nothing fit.

Raymond ran his hands over the surface of the door, leaned forward to press his face against the cool metal, surprised he had never realized how thick it was. "Eugene," he called, softly, "Eugene." He tapped with his fingertips, nails ringing on the plate of steel. Then, after a long silence, he rammed the door with his shoulder and cried out at the pain.

The door opened, just a crack, and a voice spoke, muffled, distant. "No one by your name lives here any longer." With a hollow click, the door sealed tight.

THE PRINCE OF SIXTH STREET

After the first letter Doug Prince began checking every item in his mail very carefully. That envelope had puzzled him the moment he saw it, small and mauve amid solicitations for gym memberships, restaurant menus, packets of discount coupons, and a delinquent dentist bill. His name and address were written in what he felt sure was a feminine hand, the "D" and the "P" much larger than the other letters, the tail of the final "e" like a slash across the paper.

Doug balanced the envelope in his palm, then brought it up to his nose and sniffed what seemed a faint perfume, or perhaps just the scent of the paper. He hesitated before opening, lifting an edge of the seal with his fingernail and pulling slowly as if it were important that he not tear it.

The sheet inside was the same color as the envelope, folded into a square. Doug placed it on a table with the apprehension that opening it would release a poison. But he sat back in the chair, the letter at arm's length, and unfolded. He found just a line written in the middle of the sheet: "Douglas, I hate you!" and a signature that might have been "Martha."

The words stunned him. He knew no Martha. Never in his life had he known any woman called Martha. And he couldn't think of anything he had ever done to make someone hate him. Usually, others—men and women—just ignored him, a presence who did not matter.

He looked closely at the envelope. It was addressed to Douglas Prince on Sixth Street, but then he realized the number was 16 not 6. He lived at 6—had for the ten years after finding a job in the city.

Sorting through the small pile of junk mail, he discovered a flyer for a new Thai restaurant and one offer of a reduced-rate gym membership were also addressed to 16. He opened the phone book and saw that he was the only Douglas Prince listed on Sixth Street at number 6. Next, he turned on his computer to search the list of Princes in the city, he the one Douglas.

He crossed the room to gaze out to the sidewalk below, as if he might see the person he sought, another man who looked like him. The twilight was fading, lights appearing in apartment windows up and down the street. On an impulse, he changed from slippers to shoes and took a jacket from the closet. He would go to number 16.

Outside, chilled by the wind, Doug almost turned back, saying aloud, "What am I doing?" But he couldn't make himself stop. For all his time on Sixth Street, he'd never looked closely at 16, now realized it was several stories higher than the other buildings, its stone front the only one free of grime, the front steps swept clean. It belonged in a much better neighborhood.

The door to the vestibule opened easily. Two rows of nameplates were set into marble on the left side, alphabetical. There was D. Prince at 7D. His finger paused over the buzzer, Doug saw the lens of a video camera pointing at his face and stopped. What would he have to say to a stranger who did no more than share his name? Then he thought of Martha's words, the hatred on the page. Why would he want to know a man like that? Doug returned to his apartment and locked the door, fixing the chain, something he had never done before.

The misdirected mail kept arriving. At first, Doug just wrote across the envelopes in large red letters "FORWARD TO 16 SIXTH STREET." Then he left a note for the mailman, asking him to check the address of any Douglas Prince mail very carefully. But with the carriers changing almost daily, none paid attention. Eventually, he took to saving up mail—magazines, catalogues, junk solicitations—for a week at a time and delivering the bundle to the marbled entranceway of number 16. But first class mail—bills, letters, anything that seemed personal—he forwarded immediately.

Each day Doug awaited another letter from Martha, but none

came. Telling himself he couldn't send on an opened envelope, he put it in a drawer in his night table, trying to imagine what the other man could have done, what woman would have written those words.

Eventually Doug 16—as he thought of his neighbor—returned the favor. Doug would find occasional packets of unimportant mail in his hallway under the row of mailboxes, and forwarded bills inside his box every few days. Doug sensed that Doug 16 was a much more precise person than he from the way he stacked and wrapped the packets and from the laser-printed forwarding labels on the first class mail. Initially, he worried something important would go astray—a check or, say, an invitation, though he rarely received any. Soon, however, he became confident that a man like Doug 16 would never be careless with even the most trivial of junk mail. Yet, despite the attention, he sensed that the other Doug found him a nuisance, begrudged him the effort on redirecting the mail.

He kept expecting to run into his counterpart one day, most likely in the entrance of one of their buildings, a stranger holding a packet of mail. But he never did. He tried to imagine Doug 16, conjured up only a picture of himself, as if a lost twin had turned up in his neighborhood.

For a time, he could not bring himself to tell people about the other man, though he had no idea why he should feel embarrassed about the coincidence. But the notion of a person called Doug Prince on the same block troubled him, the possibility that Doug was the man he should have been. He even dreamed of arriving home late one evening to find another man sitting in his chair, wearing his pajamas, crumpling Martha's letter in his hand and touching a match to it, the paper flaring and then scattering ashes.

Doug tried to make of joke of it, revealing the story to coworkers. "Talk about a small world," he would laugh as he reported the situation. People in the office were amused, playing along. Laura suggested that he bring the other Doug in to share his workload. But Art said that could be a problem because they would have to split Doug's salary. At lunch Tom asked what the other man looked like. "I wouldn't know if I stepped on him," he said. "Are you sure that isn't what you want to do?" Tom said. For a few weeks Doug received teasing email messages signed "The Other Doug." But then the office jokesters went on to something new.

Doug began to think about moving. Sixth Street wasn't in an affluent neighborhood, the shops in the area dreary, cluttered little holes-in-the-wall selling food and staples. The apartments themselves were small, the rooms cramped, the ceilings low. For years he had told himself he would relocate as soon as he could afford it, but he never received a promotion and never actually got around to applying for a new job as much as he read the employment ads. He wondered what Doug 16 did for a living, why he had moved to a much more elegant building on that street. The rent must have been high, Doug 16 a much more successful man.

Soon the phone calls began. The first came from telemarketers, men and woman reading haltingly from prepared scripts, some with accents, asking if he were Mr. D. Prince. At first, he tried to explain the confusion, then, when the calls kept coming, just hung up.

One evening, it was a woman on the line. "Douglas? Is that you, Doug?" Doug immediately liked the voice—soft, musical, almost pleading. He pictured an attractive woman with dark eyes, the phone held in long, tapered fingers. And he knew she hadn't called for him. No woman spoke his name that way.

"This is Doug Prince," he said, sure his own voice would make her aware that she had the wrong man.

But it didn't. "Doug, I've been trying to reach you for so long."

"Who is this?"

"It's Martha." She seemed hurt that he had to ask, on the edge of tears.

He almost cried out, It couldn't be. You hate Doug Prince, but instead spoke slowly. "I think you have the wrong Doug Prince. There are two of us on Sixth Street. We get each other's mail."

"Douglas, I know who you are."

"I'm another person. Someone else."

"Please don't lie to me."

"The Doug Prince you want is at number 16. I'm at 6."

"Doug. Please." Now she was crying

He sat frozen until he heard only silence and whispered, "I'm sorry." His hand trembled as he hung up.

Alone in the silent room, he wished he could have found words to speak to her. She sounded so lovely, so vulnerable. But what would he have said? What difference would that have made? He was the wrong man.

He believed she must have loved him, loved the other Doug. But why didn't she have his phone number? What kind of man would deny a woman like her?

Very late two nights later, a ringing woke Doug from his dozing. He fumbled with the receiver, dropped it on the night table, groped to find the right button. By the time he put it to his ear, the woman was cursing: "Goddamn you, Doug! Damn you, damn you, damn you!"

"Who is this?"

But the woman ignored him. "I can't take this any more. You've got to stop. You've got to leave me alone!"

"Martha? Is this Martha?" Doug said.

"Bastard!" The woman cut him off.

It couldn't have been Martha. This woman was shrill. But perhaps it was—Martha distraught, desperate. Or it could have been a rival, outraged at the sound of Martha's name. Yes, the more he thought about it, he was sure it wasn't Martha.

Saturday morning, Doug slept late, still exhausted after nine hours, though he had spent a slow week at the office. This time when the phone rang, even before he said "Yes," he knew who it was, and she identified herself at once: "Doug, this is Martha."

"Truly, I'm not the Doug you want," he told.

"I wish I could believe that."

"What am I supposed to look like?" he asked.

"You're tall. Strong. Thin but very strong. And very handsome. Thick black hair and deep dark eyes." She drew out the words, soft and breathless.

Doug shook his head. "I'm nothing like that. I'm not tall and certainly not handsome."

"Please don't do this."

"Martha, why do you hate Doug Prince?"

He could hear her gasp. "You know, you know, you know . . ."

"Martha, did you call the other night and tell him to stop?"

"That wasn't me." And she was gone.

Doug dreamt about her, imagining her tap on the door, the joy in her smile when he opened to let her in.

For the next week she did not call again, though the phone did ring several times with no one replying when he answered. "Martha?" he said to the silence, "Martha?" But there was nothing.

Doug decided what he had to do—confront the other man about her He took to lingering on the sidewalk after his return from work, rushing home to walk up and down the block, waiting for a tall, handsome man to approach number 16. Yet it wasn't until the next Sunday morning that he discovered him, coming out of a tiny bakery dressed in a blue blazer and red tie, taking long strides, as if he were in a hurry to be somewhere.

Doug blocked his path. "Are you Doug Prince?"

The man stared at him as if he might knock him off the sidewalk with a swipe of his hand. "Who the hell are you?"

Doug could not tell him, could not bring himself to speak his own name. Instead he said, "I have a message from Martha. She wants you to call her. Very badly."

The other Doug, Doug 16, gave out a single sound, harsh. "Martha? Martha hates me. She'd like to kill me."

"You're wrong. It's not like that."

Doug 16 gave him a quizzical look. "How do you know Martha?"

"I don't know her at all." Doug turned and ran around a corner to the avenue, not looking behind, unable to go back to Sixth Street, not wanting the man to see him enter number 6.

He returned to his apartment after dark, unlocking the door as the phone rang. With a rush he picked it up, eager to tell what he had done. But it was the other one, the shouter: "You bastard! Bastard! Stay out of my life!"

"You're not Martha," he insisted, saying it again even after the woman was no longer on the line.

Unwilling to meet Doug 16 on the street again, Doug stayed inside as much as possible, shopping near his office, carrying the packages on the bus.

One evening, he had to work late to finish a project with Laura. "Whatever happened to your namesake?" Laura asked him during a break for coffee. "That's all over," he told her.

On the way home, he saw in the streetlight that shone directly on number 16 the other man in running clothes at the top of the stone steps. Doug shrank into a shadow. Then he heard a woman call, "Doug, Doug," footsteps hurrying on the sidewalk. "Oh, Doug." It had to be Martha's voice.

Doug 16 came down the stairway, slowly, hands held out as if for protection. For a second, Doug hoped she would kill him, suddenly draw a knife and plunge it into the man's heart. Instead she fell into his arms, and his hands closed around her. Illuminated by the light, she was lovely, the Martha he had imagined. And they kissed, Martha and Doug 16, a passionate kiss so intense it made Doug shudder.

He turned away, not looking back, refusing to see more. When he got inside his apartment he sat in the dark, hat and coat still on, sat unmoving for hours. In the morning, he was the one to burn Martha's letter, certain he was the man she hated.

For several weeks mail still came for Douglas Prince at number 16. But Doug destroyed it all, tearing each one in half and half again, shoving the scraps into a black plastic bag that he knotted and stuffed into a garbage can. The packets he found in his hallway he would not read, stacking them all on a table and refusing to open. Eventually, he received no more mail for the Doug Prince at 16 and all forwarding to him stopped. The other man had left. He was the only Prince on Sixth Street.

HIS MOTHER'S CHILD

When he rounded the corner of his house on the river and saw Claudine lying on the grass, Vaughn's first instinct was to shout, "Put that thing out!" But he knew she would just suck hard and hold it in her mouth, lips pursed, no smoke emerging. Then she would swallow as if to spite him. He imagined the slight tightening of her throat muscles. In fact, he said nothing and she did not move, the joint held in two fingers of a hand that rested on her breast, her eyes closed, fingers of the other hand reaching back into the flaming red hair spread out behind her. An explosion of red on the dark green of the grass.

From where he stood Vaughn couldn't see the baby though he knew it lay beside her in a yellow bunting that matched her sweater, the soft curls of his hair already as red as hers. The boy was all Claudine, without hints of Vaughn's son, James, in his face, nor of him or Almeda, as if the child had no father, no paternal lineage.

The girl—young woman—kept the child with her constantly, rarely let anyone else hold him and hovered whenever Almeda pleaded for the opportunity, hands held out like claws, ready to snatch him back. "That's enough," she would say. Vaughn had never seen her pass the boy to James, even when he offered to help, to relieve her. "Not now," she always told him. "I'm not ready."

Yet they had given her a home, made no objection when Vaughn and James and Almeda collected her at the hospital the morning after she had given birth. "Where will you go?" Almeda had asked her before the delivery, when the girl lay on a gurney, a white sheet covering the mound of her middle. "I have no idea," she had answered, very calmly as if it were not a problem.

Out in the waiting room Vaughn had shaken his head when Almeda told him they had to bring her to their home. "I don't think that's such a good idea." And he had turned to James for an affirmation, but James sat stunned, staring out at a blank green wall, as if he were witnessing an accident. "It's James' baby," Almeda had said. "Our grandchild."

Vaughn never called the girl anything to her face, Red when he spoke about her to Almeda and James, even though Almeda each time told him, "Her name is Claudine." When they were alone, he would ask Almeda, "How long?" And Almeda gave a silent shrug that reminded him of a whimper.

He wished Claudine would stay in her room, what for years had been the guest room, next to theirs at the other end of the hallway from James'. But most of the time she spent with them in the kitchen or living room, lurking he called it, rarely speaking, her only sounds the whispers to the baby she cradled in her arms. The baby was just as quiet, except for the occasional times it screamed half the night, Vaughn furious, wrapping a pillow around his head.

A jon boat emerged from behind a cluster of trees at a bend in the river, silently propelled by an electric motor, sun glinting off the aluminum hull. Two fishermen sat with rods across their knees on their way to another place, where the fish were. Vaughn could hear the murmur of their voices but not make out any words. Claudine did not open her eyes, though he was sure she wasn't sleeping.

In frustration he moved toward her, kicking his sandals at the grass, trying to make noise. He squatted beside her, then—when his knees ached—sat with his legs folded in front of him. The marijuana odor drifted toward his face, and he turned away. Inside the house with the family she smoked only cigarettes, saved the joints for the seclusion of her room. It didn't matter. The pungency filled the air.

Almeda never referred to it, though once, in her reticent way, she had asked when the living room was thick with cigarette smoke, "Do you think that's good for the baby?" And Claudine had responded with half a laugh. "Oh, it's all right." Vaughn had tried to speak to James about it—"Can't you get her to stop?"—and it was as if he had slapped his son's face. At last James said, "I can't get her to do anything."

Here on the grass only a few feet away, Vaughn wondered what would happen if he reached out and snatched the joint from her fingers, ground it into the dirt. But all he did was say, "If you really loved that baby, you wouldn't do that."

She swept her free hand through her red hair, spread it fuller on the grass behind her, eyes still closed. Vaughn watched her closely, felt his own fingers moving in tandem with hers. Then, as he knew she would, she drew deeply on the joint, rolled the smoke in her mouth, and then released it through her curved tongue.

"It makes me feel good."

"And your child's health?"

"He's much better off with a mother who's happy."

"Can't you be happy just being a mother?"

"This makes me even happier. Much happier."

"So your happiness matters more than anything else."

Her eyes still closed, she pointed the glowing tip of the joint at him, punctuating her words with up and down gestures. "No, his does. We all show our love in different ways."

As if in response, the baby let out an open-mouthed sound, not a cry, more like an exclamation of surprise at finding himself alive in the world. His eyes opened wide and, for a few seconds, his arms and legs thrashed in the yellow bunting. Claudine handed Vaughn the joint without asking if he would take it. Her hands free, she lifted the boy high over her head and smiled at his wiggling. She brought him down to lie on her chest, closing an arm around his back and touching her lips to the fine curls of his hair. Then she gestured to Vaughn to return the joint. He hesitated, rolling the paper between thumb and forefinger.

"Take a hit," she told him.

He shook his head and passed it to her outstretched hand.

"Were you always such a puritan?"

"I don't need it."

"But James does. You've set a very bad example for your son. He's wound so tight I keep waiting for the last twist that will make him explode. Shards of James flying in all directions."

Vaughn gestured toward the baby now breathing softly on his mother's chest. "Is he really James' son?"

"Don't you mean really your grandson?"

"It's the same thing."

"Technically."

"Well?"

She brought the joint to her lips, sucked a deep hit, and emitted the smoke with a hiss through her teeth. Vaughn took it as a gesture of mockery.

"James is much more his mother's child," she said.

He felt a throb of real anger. "What has that got to do with it?"

"He's afraid of me. You must know that. He taps on the door to my room, whispers my name, and then waits. It's like begging. Maybe he should try marching right in."

"And then what?"

"We'd have to find out, wouldn't we?"

Vaughn wanted to slap the joint from her fingers, slap the expression off her face.

To his surprise, she reached the baby out to him, the boy dangling from her hands, his face quivering as if about ready to release a wailing. For an instant Vaughn was ready to stand up and walk away, but he leaned forward and accepted the child, gripped him under his arms and pulled him up to his shoulder, one hand cushioning his padded bottom. The wetness had seeped through the diaper into the fleece of the bunting. He knew he could return the boy to Claudine in a manner that would rebuke her mothering. But he wrapped him tighter, felt the child relax in his grip, the red curls brushing under his chin. He touched his fingertips to the boy's face, felt the warm flesh.

"Grandpa," she said.

"Am I?" He wanted to love the child, sure he would tremble with a rush of emotion if she said yes.

"Then," she said, "we would have a real connection. A permanent one."

"Don't we?" The baby gulped and emitted a strand of white spittle that ran down Vaughn's throat.

Claudine didn't answer. She closed her eyes and lay back on the grass, stretched her arms wide, and flicked away the stub of the joint. Vaughn stared down at her face trying to read her emotions but found only an opaque calm.

He leaned forward to place the baby on her, bracing himself with a hand that came down in the rich red hair fanned behind her head, his fingers tangled in the strands. Her expression did not change. Her eyes did not flutter. Still he suspected she knew what he was doing. He wondered what would happen if he yanked on her hair, if he knotted it in his fist. But he didn't. He just stayed as immobile as she and waited for her to move first.

STEINWAY AND THE WIZARD

They spoke to her endlessly, all night and all day, Steinway and the Wizard, Steinway an almost-dwarf of a man, fat, jowled, grey-fleshed. The Wizard lived in shadow, at times a feature revealed in a slant of light. But he never appeared whole. She knew he was very tall, his lips thin and bloodless, his eyes so deep and dark they seemed pits of blackness. Only his hands were vivid, rings flashing so brightly each gesture made her dizzy. His voice startled—harsh, snarling, quaking at an edge of fury. She dreaded the sound of it. Steinway's sound was soft, as flabby as the rest of him, pouring over her like a viscous oil.

When Steinway or the Wizard spoke, her head burned; she would seize fistfuls of hair and tug at her scalp to make them stop. Yet, she always ached to listen. What they said was important.

Steinway told her secrets, facts she had always suspected but had not allowed herself to think until he made them real. Secrets about her parents, her husband, her children, about Maribel—all the deceivers. His words made their treachery clear, and now she was desperate to defeat the people who had betrayed her.

The Wizard shared no information; he shouted imperatives, assumed she knew everything, cursed her when she did not. He swore foulmouthed: goddamn fucking whore bitch! His anger was so intense she felt her head shattering from the force of it. Many times the pressure made her smash things to relieve the blasts of his ranting, hurl glass against the walls, stab scissors into furniture. The Wizard was a raw nerve of rage. He commanded and she was compelled to obey.

Steinway told her too much. He claimed to have chosen her alone because he wanted to help. But he left her nothing. At times she would clamp her hands to her ears to shut him out; still his words lived inside her. She would have to rip out her brain to stop him. His truths made her shriek. Now she knew: husband, parents, brother, sister, children, liars who were stealing her life. Whenever one of them called, she let the phone ring seven times—no more, no less—and held the receiver in silence while the caller uttered her name; then she slammed it into the cradle and damned them all.

She had loved them once, and the memory of that love brought her to tears, moments of sobbing so violent she had to curl up on the carpet. They were all betraying her; they submitted to Maribel now, servile before her greatest enemy. And she hated them all the more because they had perverted her love.

Her husband was not to be trusted. She had almost screamed the first time Steinway told her that, clinging flat to the bed, squeezing the pillow in her hands, nauseated from the pounding of her heart. Her husband was not to be trusted. Even though she had wept when Steinway told her, she had accepted the revelation at once. To know explained everything. Her husband was a fraud. Of course. Of course. She should not believe a word he said.

They were all evil people. She had suspected it for such a long time, but Steinway gave her evidence. Her husband had murdered his mother, filled her with cancer germs. He would kill her too if she did not resist him. Her parents were monsters. They had stood in darkness beyond the circle of light to watch when her husband made the butchers castrate her.

Until Steinway told her the truth, she had believed Maribel responsible for her castration. That was what Maribel had wanted her to think. I'm more of a woman that you, Maribel repeated day after day, through the darkness of the nights, preening as if before a mirror, extending short, thick legs as if she were beautiful. You tried to be better than me, and I've fixed you. I had them cut away your sensations.

But Steinway confided with an oozing murmur that Maribel only wished she had been his chosen one. Maribel hated her. But Maribel had no power; she possessed nothing but hatred. It was he, her husband, who had condemned her to the butcher.

The Wizard shrilled commands of vengeance, urged her to the knives racked in the pantry. It would be justice; it would be right. Each time she looked down at her sleeping husband, she shuddered at his vulnerability.

She stood over him a knife in each hand, while Maribel coaxed in a chant—Good, good, do it now. And she was terrified. Why wasn't the Wizard the one to tell her? What if Maribel was disobeying the Wizard? Her head burned with possibilities. She fell to the floor and stretched out flat, stiff, face pressed down against the hard boards, the knives red hot along her sides.

What was right? What was true? She had no power to question; she could only listen. Steinway gave nothing but the information he chose to tell. And she dared not approach the Wizard. He would roar outrage, force the most awful punishments.

She lay on the floor, totally rigid. Perhaps if she held herself still enough, long enough, they would all forget her. No one would speak; she would hear none of the voices. The silence would be bliss. Husband and parents and brother and sister and children would never see her again; she would never have to see anyone again. And Steinway and the Wizard and Maribel would vanish. She herself would evaporate in the silence and become nothing.

She held her breath to savor the absolute quiet. But Maribel laughed out loud, mouth gaping in a frantic cackling: The Wizard is mine. No matter what you believe, I am the one he loves. When I truly ask, he will make you plunge the knives.

She rolled onto her back and stared out at the slit of moon that sliced the darkness, her body writhing with dread, as she awaited the next command.

REVERSE

"Why are we here?" Michelle's eyes were dazed. "Because it's not there."

Louis dragged their luggage, a single duffle bag, through the terminal, his free hand splayed in the center of her back, bunching the cloth of her blouse, forcing her through the crowd. During the landing she had seized the vomit bag, holding it under her chin, but just spitting and dropping her head against the seat back. Now her face was ashen, her hair matted with sweat.

Outside, under a grey sky, a wind swirled a chill drizzle. He hoisted the duffle bag onto his shoulder and seized her arm, pulling her out into the roadway. "Run!"

"Louis, I'm exhausted."

"I said run."

When they reached the auto rental building, she collapsed on a bench blotting her forehead while he negotiated, slaming the duffle bag onto the floor tiles, angry because they had no cars with automatic transmission. The clerk, a plain woman with a severe haircut, recited an apology as she listed the alternatives, her English unpleasantly nasal.

"Anything," he said. "Just get me away from this place."

She tapped at her computer and the printer hummed, ejecting forms for him to sign. He scrawled his name and snatched the keys from her fingers.

When Louis found the small grey vehicle in the lot, a Renault Clio, he unlocked Michelle's door and pushed her into the seat. Rainwater dripped from her hair, ran down her face. He drove straight from the parking slot onto the exit road, roaring the engine in second gear, cursing because he had forgotten how to shift.

The road signs indicated that they were moving away from the city. "Can't we stop there?" Michelle sighed. "Find a hotel?"

"I want to get away from people."

"What people?"

"You know what people."

"He's three thousand miles away. On the other side of an ocean, for God's sake."

"That's not good enough."

He had not told her they were going, just appeared home late the morning before and ordered her to lay out clothes for packing. The arrangements were already made, the tickets in his jacket. He wouldn't let her call anyone, not even to cancel a doctor's appointment: "They'll know when you don't show up." The cab came minutes later, and all the way to the airport she had wept in the back seat.

"It's not why you think," she had told him, sniffling back her tears.

"Why then?"

"Because we live this way."

"I didn't choose it. It wasn't I who betrayed you."

Although their ages were fifteen years apart, Louis looked much older with his thin grey hair, his sagging chins, his sunken eyes. He moved with a round-shouldered stoop as if he had shrunk in the five years of their marriage. Michelle wasn't beautiful, even pretty, but she wore clothes that accentuated her slimness, hair styles that flattered her broad face. People congratulated him on finding an attractive woman so soon after his divorce.

Then, a week ago, home unexpectedly early from a business trip, he watched a car, low and sleek, pull into the driveway, Michelle lean over and give the driver a quick kiss on the lips. But Louis couldn't see the man, his face blurred by the sun glare on the windshield.

After hours of driving, when Michelle's protested that she was hungry, needed the toilet, became a shrill pleading, he pulled off at an inn on a hill high above the highway, snaking up a gravel drive and parking at the edge of a sheer drop, facing the mountains to the west, their dark stone streaked with gashes of snow, their peaks smothered in cloud.

They ate in silence, forks clattering on their plates, Michelle looking down at the tabletop, Louis glaring at her the whole time.

When they went to the toilets, he used the men's room quickly and stood at the door to the ladies', clamping a hand on her elbow the moment she came out. "Let's go."

She tried to shake him off, but he squeezed until she gasped.

When the stranger's car backed out of the drive, Louis was already standing in the hallway. Michelle cried out when she opened the door and saw him looming, his face fierce, an arm held over his head like a club. Her purse dropped to the tiles, splitting apart like a wound.

"Tell me his name," he had demanded.

"Mark."

She knelt, gathering spilled coins, lipstick, a compact, replacing the items one by one. "His name is Mark."

"How long?"

"Not long."

"How long?" This time he roared the question.

"A month. Six weeks."

"And what do you expect to happen?"

"I don't know. I don't think about the future."

"Maybe there is none."

In their car outside the inn Louis sat for a long time before turning on the engine, staring out at the dark mountains, the thick grey sky, then studied the pattern on the shift knob up and to the right for reverse. But when he pushed, the lever seemed blocked. He forced the knob down and tried again, then pulled it up. Neither method worked. Each time he tried, he let the clutch out slowly, and the car inched forward toward the brink of the drop.

"Goddamn fucking sonofabitch!" He stomped the clutch pedal, shifted through the forward gears, angrily, violently, then rammed the lever upward, but couldn't make it go into reverse.

"Do you want me to get out and push the car back?" Michelle closed her fingers on the door handle.

"Shut up!

"I can't drive a car like this."

An elderly couple who had been eating at the next table appeared on the path, sinewy people with stiff grey hair and veined arms. Michelle rolled down her window. "We can't find reverse." Her voice was desperate.

When they gave her blank looks, she pointed to the shift lever, then gestured behind the car, shrugged her exasperation.

The couple conversed in their language, a clipped singsong, until the woman smiled and said, "Ahh." The man motioned to Michelle that she should step out. He sat next to Louis and reached down to the shift lever, gripping a metal ring inside the leather sheath and lifting it upward; then the lever slid easily into reverse. He took Louis' fingers in his hand and guided him through a demonstration.

Louis nodded that he understood. Michelle thanked the couple very much, put on a broad smile, waved the whole time they got into their own car and drove away.

In neutral, Louis pressed the gas pedal to the floor, held it until the car shuddered and black smoke surged from the exhaust.

Though the night after he discovered the man in the driveway, Louis had demanded explanations, sat Michelle on the sofa and wouldn't let her sleep, shook her awake when her eyes drooped.

"Is he married too?"

"Not any more?"

"What do you tell him about this marriage?"

"That I'm very unhappy."

"And he's sympathetic? Overflowing with compassion?"

"Yes."

"Do you love him?"

"I need someone like him."

"You'll never have him. Do you understand? I will take you so far from here that you'll never see him again."

Her face had collapsed with sobbing, so distorted that he found her very ugly.

"I should have gone over the edge." Louis muttered. "A quick end."

Michelle huddled against the door, hands wrapped in her seat belt. "If I promise . . . If I swear never to see him again, can we go home?"

"How could I trust a woman like you? What's to stop you and your Mark from rushing off together to some secret place?"

"There's nowhere to hide."

"Baloney. We're hiding now, aren't we?"

"Not from you."

"I wish I could believe that," he said.

The road up to the mountain top was hard, rutted dirt, a single lane, knotted with switchbacks, dark valleys plunging below. Though it was warm when they started the climb, far above them deep snow filled the crevices between the peaks.

"Be careful," Michelle said. "Please."

"Lives like ours are nothing but risks."

He wrenched the steering wheel to hug the rockface. Few cars were on the road, several far behind them, one or two up ahead. When one appeared from around a sharp bend, moving downhill, Louis had to swerve into a bypass, his hands trembling, waiting until the car was long past, unable to turn around, hesitant to start climbing again.

But he moved forward, gaining speed on a straight stretch, then slamming over a bump that knocked the transmission into neutral. The engine vibrated with a furious whine and they went nowhere.

"It's overheating." Michelle pointed at the temperature needle wavering up near the red line.

He rammed into first gear with a clash of metal. "An explosion. You and me in a great ball of fire." The car lurched ahead.

She shut her eyes, shook her head again and again.

"Make yourself look," he demanded, gesturing at the deep dark valleys below. "It's a shame to miss the drama of the view."

The days before they left the country, Louis followed her. Michelle would glance up from the aisle of a store and find him across from her, glaring, his face an accusation. He would tell her he had appointments at his office, then appeared in the kitchen, announcing, "They were cancelled. Everything was cancelled." Finally, she hid in the bedroom, closing the door, refusing to leave. He left her meals in the hallway, tapping on the wood and then drawing back to the stairs, waiting to see her eyes when she reached for the food.

Loose rocks battered the underside of the Renault, scattering off the edge of the road as the back tires slid though an abrupt turn.

"What did you two do?" Louis said, teeth clenched as he gripped the wheel.

"Can't we talk about it later? When we're there."

"Where's there?"

"Wherever we're going."

"Who knows where that is. All this is new to me. Mysterious territory."

"It's so dangerous. Let's wait. Please." She was gripping the seat cushion, digging her nails into the fabric.

"Now. I want to know now."

"You don't want to hear." She was crying again, inward sobs that racked her body.

"Now!"

"We did everything you think we did."

"I think you told him how much you loved your husband."

"Oh, God! How could I?"

"I think you told him that you and I … we couldn't live without each other."

When the car pounded into deep rut, shuddered with a crack of metal, Michelle screamed.

The road widened when they reached an open space, facing an expanse of dark rock and snow-covered peaks. Louis pulled up into the row of cars beside a square granite building. A grey haze hung over the ground, blocked the distant views. It was as if they had driven into a cloud.

Three people appeared at the door to the inn, bundled in parkas, hoods drawn tight around their faces, hands huge in thick mittens. A woman let out a cry as they dashed to their car.

"It must be frigid outside," Louis said. He was wearing a short-sleeved shirt, thin, pale arms prickled with chill.

Michelle tugged her linen jacket tighter, hugged herself and shivered. "What is this place?" she said.

"A lodge. People come here for warmth."

"Let's go back."

"Back where?"

"Anywhere."

"There's no back for us. Only what happens next."

"What? Tell me!"

He shrugged. "We'll both know when it happens."

Louis made her get out. When she opened the car, icy winds sliced through them. Michelle ran toward the lodge, stumbling, hair swirling, while Louis walked behind gritting his teeth at the pain of the cold.

The door slammed behind him and people stared, the woman behind a wooden counter, the people clustered at tables in the small dining area, the waitress, the teenagers on benches surrounding a fireplace. Michelle hurried to stand in front of the flames, spreading her arms and leaning toward the heat.

The entranceway was crammed with backpacks, pack racks, skis, and boots. A moose head was mounted high on a brick wall, broad antlers and glazed eyes.

Louis motioned Michelle to sit at a small brown table. He ordered bread, cheese, and coffee, challenging the scrutiny of the others, men and women in thick sweaters; one lone man in bright red nodded to him, holding up a glass as if in a toast, dark-haired, handsome.

"Can we take a room, Louis?" Michelle begged. "Just for a few hours. I'm so tired I feel sick."

"Is that him?"

"Who?"

"That man. Is that your Mark?"

Michelle turned to follow Louis's eyes, and the man in red smiled. She looked away quickly. "Mark's nothing like that."

"Of course, you can say that. You can say anything."

"How could Mark know we're here? How could anybody?"

"How could I hope to know all your secrets?"

"There aren't any more." She balled a napkin in her hands, shredded the paper. "Please believe me."

"It's too late for that."

Back in the car, Michelle removed two sweaters from the duffle, pulling one atop the other. Louis studied a map. "We could go back down the way we came or take another route, one that's barely a line on the paper, without even a number."

"Anything. Let's just get away from here."

"I choose the unknown way. Who knows what we'll find."

They coasted down a long incline, Louis riding with a foot on the brake, pumping the entire way. Then the road spiraled upward, very narrow, barely wide enough for the Renault.

Snow coated the ground, drifted against boulders, weighed down the limbs of the trees, at first just a coating, but growing deeper as they climbed, so white it dazzled even in the greyness of this day. Louis had to squint to see.

Snow swirled across the windshield, but Louis couldn't tell if it were a new fall or just blown by the wind. He saw no other cars, none behind and none ahead, no signs of life.

"No one comes this way," he said. "We're discovering virgin territory. Pure white. Like a bride."

"Let's turn around. Go back on the other road."

"How? Where? Once you take this route, there's no escape."

Now snowbanks rose on both sides of the road, as high as the car, thin poles rising far above them, evenly spaced, marking the bends of the path.

"I can't see!" Michelle was crying. "How can you drive!"

"I go where the road should be. But life is filled with surprises."

"I couldn't help it. I didn't mean to fall in love with Mark."

"Then how can you expect me to be in control of myself?"

The snow deepened, almost reaching the tips of the poles now, looming above them under a leaden sky, as if they were moving through a tunnel.

Then, as they rounded a curve, the road widened, and Louis relaxed his grip on the steering wheel, until he saw headlights appear from the other direction. He had forgotten to turn on his own, groping for the switch as the other car closed in, moving much too fast.

Louis slammed the brakes, swerved toward the snow, just as the car passed. A loud snapping noise resounded, and then there was silence.

Michelle cringed against the passenger door, feet up on the seat, hugging her face to her knees. He got out to see the damage, found no marks on the side of the car before he realized the side mirror was missing, torn loose and lying in the center of the road like a dead animal.

The other car had stopped too, gleaming black. The driver stepped onto the road, long legs in fur-lined boots, dark-haired, wearing a red sweater like the man in the lodge.

"Quick! Look!" Louis reached inside and dragged Michelle across the seat, pulled her out onto the road. "Is that one him? Is that your Mark?"

"I wish it was."

"Would Mark save your life?"

"Yes."

"Then go to him. I don't want you any more."

Louis slammed the door and drove off, her scream louder than the wind. He fixed his gaze on the spot where the side mirror had been, refusing to turn his head, to look behind, unwilling to know if Michelle was moving toward the man in red.

UNDER THE DECK

What the people on the deck have in common?

The world. They had been all over the world, sharing experiences of places that most people had barely heard of, able to name a city a street a restaurant a hotel a lake a mountain and know that the others would envision the same memory. "Oh yes," someone would say. "The wine, the cobblestones, the church bells in the towers, the statues in the park, the buildings that seemed to grow out of the hillsides." Bungee jumping from a helicopter in New Zealand, enjoying string quartets in Aix en Provence, play reading in San Miguel Allende, boarding the TGV at Lausanne, climbing with a guide in Nepal, meeting for drinks on the Lido, booking a suite at the Imperial Hotel in Tokyo.

Where were they at that moment?

Sitting in cushioned chairs on the deck of a country home, drinking espresso, sipping Cointreau or Vin Santo and passing plates of airy sweets, watching the brilliant sunset over the lake, hearing the breeze rustling through the leaves, listening to the sudden trill of bird songs, someone holding up a finger, cocking an ear to bring a pause to the conversation.

How did they feel?

Delightful. That was the word used by Valerie: "It's delightful here." She sighed, spread her arms, and looked up at the glow of the quarter moon. "Yes, it's wonderful," Arthur said. "Good food, good wine," Thomas added. "And good friends." Leslie raised her glass. "Hmmm," the others said as they joined her in a hum of pleasure.

How did they come to be together?

Several had been neighbors at one time. Others had met long ago through professional associations. Three were the children of the original group of friends, having gathered like this since they were toddlers, now out of college, beginning their own successes, at ease with each other, with their elders, speaking fondly of those who were not there this day, off to some distant place, storing adventures to share the next time they all came together.

Why were they here?

The occasion was purely social, an opportunity stimulated by a holiday weekend, a break from the long hours of their careers, organized by phone calls from the hosts, Andre and Eleanor. "We'll be at the lake," they had said, "and guess who else is coming," as if enticements were necessary with the promise of fine wines, excellent food, and fascinating people.

Whose holiday was it? The nation's. It was a national holiday. That was part of their amusement, though no one spoke of it. But they knew what the others were thinking. For a number of them—couples, whole families, or just the husband or the wife—this was not their country. They had been born elsewhere: Edinburgh, Hong Kong, Lillehammer, Vancouver, Johannesburg. Yet they had lived here for years, owned homes, businesses and practices. None knew which of the others was or wasn't a citizen. The question never came up. They had raised a toast at dinner—"Happy Holiday"—smiled and touched glasses.

How many were gathered on the deck?

About a dozen of them. The number changed from one moment to the next, Andre and Eleanor moving back and forth into the house for another carafe of coffee, another bottle of liqueur, another plate of sweets, the young people coming and going, three there now, some already off to parties with other friends, more due to arrive, Annalise and Giancarlo, driving directly from the airport when their flight from Rome landed.

Where was Carl Muntz?

Under the deck, back against a wooden piling, hugging a brown paper bag to his chest, teeth chattering despite the mellow summer evening, limbs shivering in trousers still soaked from losing his foothold at the edge of the lake. He tried to hold himself absolutely still, pressing his lips together, aware of the rasping of his quick shallow breaths, freezing when the people above him paused to listen to the song of a bird, though he had no idea of the reason for the sudden quiet, certain it was he; that he had made a noise that would give him away, still unsure what would happen to his plan if one of them climbed down to the grass and crouched to look under the wooden platform, how he would react if a stranger's eyes locked on to his.

How had Carl Muntz gotten there?

By boat from across the lake, from the area where the bank was steep and the brambles grew thick, unsuitable for building, a tangle of reeds at the water's edge, heavy tree limbs dragging the surface.

Where did he find the boat?

He stole it from the yard of an empty cottage fifty yards away from the trees, an old green rowboat that smelled of rot, upside down on two sawhorses and fixed to a tree by a rusted chain that he twisted until it snapped. Then he dragged the boat across the grass into the water, soaking his shoes for the first time, his trousers to the knees.

Why this lake?

For years he had come here to escape the town, to lie under the sun on the grassy bank and pretend he was the only human being in the world. That was before people like Andre and Eleanor built their vacation homes and spoiled his place. He had avoided the lake for three years, but this day could think of nowhere else to be.

How had he come to be under this deck?

By chance. When Carl Muntz rowed across to the south side of the lake, he slipped on a rock stepping out and plunged thigh deep into the water. He pushed the empty boat back toward the center and scanned the row of large houses set back on broad sweeping lawns. On an impulse he chose this one, lured by the sunset's jagged glare on the upper windows. When he reached the bank he ran, feeling the water squish in his shoes, panting open-mouthed, tumbling onto his side and rolling under the deck.

Had he planned to stay there?

No. His intention had been to find a way into the house. But before he could gather himself together and seek an entrance, the French doors opened and people came outside, laughing, praising the evening's beauty, clinking cups and saucers, holding cognac glasses, their footsteps jarring the wood above his head.

Why was he there?

To ruin. To give pain. To obliterate these people and their house, wishing it could be all the people and all the houses on this side of the lake. To make them know what it was like to be him. In the brief seconds of their excruciating torment to feel all of his miserable years. From the moment he fled the motel that evening he had ached to spread his anguish.

How did he feel at that moment?

Frantic, agitated, his chest craving a cigarette, his muscles in spasm from the strain of holding himself still. He smelled his wrath like a rancid crust that coated his flesh, wondered how those above could be ignoring the stink of him.

Did he listen to their conversations?

Barely. He was much too busy revising his plan, trying to decide what to do next now that he had not gotten into the house. What he did hear confused him. City names that meant nothing to him, resorts and villages and hotels. For a moment he wondered how they could have seen so many places, but then remembered that this was the last place they would ever see. At the thought, his heart thumped like a huge drum beating in the night.

Where had Carl Muntz been in his life?

Nowhere was what he would have said, though, of course, he had been somewhere, though rarely very far from the town of his birth, not much farther than he could drive in an hour or two, always to places that looked little different from the one he had always known, the narrow row houses, the old cars lined at the curb, crowded into cinder driveways, the grey factories with smokestacks that billowed black clouds into the sky.

Was he impressed by the sophistication of the people on the deck?

He hated them. He had not known who he would find on this side of the lake, what the people who lived in these great vacation homes were like. But now that he heard their voices, their sounds of happiness, their soft laughter, he truly loathed them.

Did he know what these people did in their lives?

He couldn't have imagined that they were physicians and professors, artists and engineers, executives and investment bankers, bibliophiles and connoisseurs. All he knew was that their lives were totally unlike his.

What did Carl Muntz do?

Sit at a table in a tiny kitchen with his aged mother and smoke cigarettes down to butts that burned his fingertips, hear his father's TV blaring down through the ceiling, watch the old lady drink an unending cup of coffee, listen to her lament his terrible jobs, at least once a day exploding with anger at the unfairness of her accusations. He tried, he had always tried, but bosses ignored him; no matter how much he busted his ass they never gave him a chance. "People don't like me!" he would shout at his mother, beat on the table until her coffee spilled.

What was Carl Muntz carrying in the brown bag?

An incendiary device, a bomb. Homemade, a volatile liquid in a glass jar, one from the shelf that his mother used for canning. The liquid was acetone, a paint thinner from the hardware store, something anyone could buy. He had filled the jar halfway, having once heard that fumes were even more explosive; but first he had punched a hole in the lid with a awl and inserted a firecracker with a long wick. Although he had never made a bomb before, wouldn't have known where to look for instructions, he had been pleased with himself while concocting it, alone in the basement, speeding there straight from the motel and telling himself that he would build a bomb even though he had never before in his life thought about a bomb.

Why did Carl Muntz make the bomb?

Fury, hatred, desperation. In the basement, he stared up at the ceiling as if to look into the narrow parlor where his parents sat, too deaf to hear his clattering, old people, their flesh sagging, joints swollen, both of them groaning with the ache of movement. As he poured the acetone into the jar, he knew he would never see them again. But they would read about him, see his picture in the newspaper. A man with a bomb. A source of ruin. A bringer of great pain.

Why didn't he blow up his own house?

It wouldn't be enough. Not his house or his parents or every house on their street, the entire neighborhood. Who would care if he destroyed people like himself, people who didn't matter?

Why had he been at a motel?

He didn't want to think about the reason, even as he waited under the deck with nothing to do but try to plan what would come next and listen to the chatter from above. Every time the scene in the motel began to enter his memory, he made himself imagine what the bomb would be like when it detonated the earsplitting blast, the searing red flash of fire, the sizzle and stench of life consumed. If he could do what he had done in the motel, why not a bomb?

What stunned him from his reverie?

The chirp of a phone, cordless, on a table directly overhead, Andre's soft "Hello," and then his happy laughter. "Annalise, I knew it had to be you. Where are you? In the car. Coming soon. Wonderful. Wait. I'll give you your mother. Marta, it's Annalise. On her mobile phone." The others were laughing too. "It's Annalise," they all said, and one voice louder than the others, a woman, excited: "Darling, how was the flight? And Giancarlo? My love to Giancarlo." There was a murmur from the others. "Everyone's love to Giancarlo. See you soon."

Did Carl Muntz return to thoughts of the bomb when Annalise's mother hung up?

No. He pictured what Annalise would look like. Tall, thin, golden bracelets on long tanned arms, her dark hair in thick waves, her lips red and moist, her black eyes flashing. Like a woman in a magazine, a model, speeding toward them in a car that smelled of soft new leather and cost more than he would earn in a lifetime. He wished it had been Annalise in the motel. But if she had been there, would he have done what he did? Yes. He nodded to himself, a gesture of certainty. It would have been perfect if Annalise had been the one in the motel.

Who was the one in the motel?

A young woman named Sharon Fahy, half his age, probably the same as Annalise, but not someone whose picture would ever be in a magazine, skinny and drab, with a long face and crooked teeth, hollow cheeks and protruding ears. For the year they had been meeting, it made Carl Muntz sad each time he looked at her, each time he drove up to the QuickChek where she cashiered. Each time she opened the passenger's door of his rusting Plymouth, then sat silently with hands folded in her lap. Each time they headed directly to the same tattered motel for sex, she passive beneath his slack weight, he thrashing frantically, hands groping at her fleshless frame, desperate for a reaction from her, some emotion that would give the act pleasure.

What were the people on the deck saying?

They spoke of Annalise. Julia, Valerie's daughter, told how they had met in Gstaad last winter for a ski break after Annalise's exhibit in Paris, both discovering that they disliked the town, the shops and cafés overflowing with overdressed people, women in fur jackets, men in leather, all glittering with jewelry and smelling of cologne. They packed up, checked out, and went to Chateau d'Oex, just ten minutes away on the train line, a town where the Swiss skied, where everyone was friendly and the food in the Café de la Gare, delicious, a tabby cat under the table winding between their legs. Then Giancarlo joined them from Milan, celebrating the completion of a major stage in his research, exuberant, dazzling in his skiing, people stopping to watch and admire.

Did Carl Muntz pay attention to her story?

To the last part, enough to imagine Giancarlo on skis, losing his balance, tripping, plunging over a ravine, landing head first on ice, his neck snapped, head wrenched at a weird angle, lifeless eyes staring up at the people gathered above him.

How did he picture Giancarlo's face?

He didn't. The face he saw was Sharon's, eyes bulging, lip swollen, blood trickling down her chin, her front tooth chipped at a spiked angle.

Why did he see her that way?

It was how she looked when he realized she was dead, the instant he removed his hands from her throat and her body stood propped against the wall panel, before it slumped forward and sprawled onto the grey carpet.

What did he do then?

He tried to replace her clothes, the jeans and the sweatshirt, hands trembling too much to attempt her underwear, then ripping the cord from a table lamp and knotting one end around her wrists, the other around her ankles. He dragged her into the bathroom and hoisted the body into the tub, turning on the water and sealing the drain. When the water covered her head, her short wiry hair bobbing on the surface, he used his shirt to wipe down the room, erase his fingerprints, even though he knew the gesture was futile. They would know he had done it. He had signed the register; the clerk had seen him every week for a year.

Why did he kill her?

Because no matter what he did he could not make her respond to him, because that night he stopped in the middle of the act and shouted at her, "Why the fuck are we doing this?" "Because I'm so lonely," she told him and began weeping. He slapped her with the back of his left hand, then punched her with his right fist. The jagged edge of the broken tooth cut into his knuckle. When she just lay there, staring up at him, not making a sound, not a gesture of defense, he turned furious, locking his hands under her chin and lifting her from the bed, forcing her against the wall, beating her head against the dark brown paneling, feeling her windpipe collapse under his thumbs.

Did he mean to kill her?

Yes. At the moment he was doing it, he wanted her dead. But if, moments before, when they were still on the bed, she had reached out to embrace him, he would have told her he loved her.

Why did he cry out now?

Someone spilled steaming coffee on the deck. First he heard a muttered "Damn," then felt the hot liquid scalding his scalp. "Fuck!" he shouted and jumped up, banging his head against the bottom of a plank. "Who's there?" a man's voice called out, and then there was silence, until a woman spoke, slowly, hesitantly: "Come out, whoever you are."

What did Carl Muntz do?

He moved quickly, eager to be out from under the deck before people climbed down and surrounded him. As he tumbled and rolled onto the grass, he held the bag with the bomb up with one hand and reached the other into his pocket for the cigarette lighter.

What did the people on the deck do?

They clustered at the railing, looking down at him, speaking excitedly to each other: "Who's that man?" "Do you know him?" "I've never seen him before." Finally, Andre, the host, called out, "Who are you? What are you doing here?"

How did Carl Muntz answer?

"I've got a bomb. Stay the fuck away from me." He flicked the lighter, shooting out an orange flame, but held it high above his head, away from the wick in the jar. He imagined the deck blown up, the bodies of these people heaped in fire, their silk tunics and plaid trousers and white cotton sweaters, their pearls and jeweled earrings ripped and twisted, smeared with blood and seared flesh.

Why didn't he throw the bomb?

He wasn't sure it would destroy. If they had been inside the house, he would have gathered them together, collected their wallets and watches and jewelry, then blown up the room, watched the building burst into flames, all of these people coughing at thick black smoke, flailing their arms at the fire, shrieking terror as the walls collapsed. But here, outdoors, there was nothing to burn, only the wood under their feet. He thought to demand that they all go inside but knew he couldn't make them do it.

What idea suddenly struck him?

Escape. Their cars lined up in the driveway alongside the house. He would take one of their cars and flee. He flicked the lighter again and cocked the jar like a football, gesturing his intention to fling it onto the deck. "Throw me your car keys," he demanded.

"All of them?" someone asked. For a second, he didn't know how to answer, then looked to see which was at the front of the drive, facing directly out to the street. "The brown one." "The BMW?" "The fucking brown one!" "That's yours, Arthur." A grey-haired man nodded, reached into the pocket of a blue blazer, and tossed a key case down onto the grass.

Did Carl Muntz get away?

Carl Muntz scooped the case up in the hand that held the lighter and ran toward the parked cars. But before he reached the edge of the grass a little round sports car swung into the driveway, bright blue, loud music throbbing from four speakers, a young couple waving happily to the people on the deck, not noticing him, not realizing that this man with a bomb even existed. The woman, Annalise, was more lovely than Carl Muntz had imagined, blonde, not dark, not tan, still someone from a magazine. It was Giancarlo who was dark and tan, tall, muscular, handsome. "Stop that man!" someone called, and Giancarlo vaulted from the car and rushed toward Carl Muntz, who wheeled about and began running toward the lake. He dropped the key case, kicked it to one side, and then stopped. Giancarlo stopped too, wary, limbs tensed, ready to pounce. As he shot out a flame from the lighter, Carl Muntz heard a woman scream. It must have been Annalise. He touched the flame to the wick in the jar, made sure it caught, a small red glow at the tip of the black cord. Then he threw the bomb at Giancarlo.

Did the bomb explode?

Yes, but not on Giancarlo, instead the instant it left Carl Muntz's hand, the impact knocking him flat, the flaming acetone raining down on him, singeing his hair, burning his face, setting his shirt on fire.

What of Giancarlo?

Giancarlo, unhurt, having leapt behind the bushes before the blast, saved Carl Muntz's life, flinging himself on top of him, rolling him over onto the lawn to smother the flames, slapping at the fire in his hair with clumps of dewy grass. He called to Annalise for the blanket from his car, wrapped Carl Muntz from neck to ankles, pried open his mouth to secure his tongue, and then pulled off his shoes.

And what of Carl Muntz?

Convulsing, limbs twitching as if shocked with strong currents, he cursed Giancarlo, spit out choked obscenities until he screamed and fainted.

Did Carl Muntz recover?

His burns were quite severe, his face disfigured, third degree on his chest and back, in need of months of skin grafts that would leave his flesh crusted and mottled, one eye sightless, his nerve endings in perpetual pain.

How was it that Giancarlo knew exactly what to do?

He was a physician and, although he now devoted his time to research, had spent enough hours in clinics to be an expert in trauma medicine.

Where were the others during Giancarlo's heroics?

Crowded at the railing of the deck, scrutinizing every gesture, a memory as they watched, silently rehearsing the words they would use to recall this adventure the next time they gathered.

STRUCTURE

Patrick was patching the village street, picking out chunks of pavement from the potholes and ladling in steaming tar, when the car went by. Even though the village was on no main route, "dead center on the way to nowhere" as the people liked to say, he usually paid little attention to the occasional strange vehicles sealed tight in their sleek speed, from a world that had nothing to do with his. But this one was peculiar—old and bloated, of a make he did not recognize, dull green, wallowing on worn shocks and fat underinflated tires. It moved slowly, swinging wide to pass him. The driver, a man with a tanned bald head, looked closely at the small pile of pavement chunks Patrick had piled at the roadside as if counting them. Patrick touched the tip of his cap but couldn't tell if the man nodded back. When the car reached the end of the village, a loose muffler struck sparks off the surface of the creek bridge. Patrick stopped his work to watch it head out onto the treeless rock-strewn landscape and disappear around the bend past the sheep grazing at the pond. "Now who'd want to drive a thing like that?" he said aloud even though no one was near enough to hear.

He watched the dark clouds layered at the horizon, shifting smears of grey. There hadn't been a day of real sun in weeks. He thought about the stranger's glowing tan and wondered where the man had come from.

The tar pot hung from a metal stand over a black burner flame, the smell so thick Patrick could feel each breath clogging his lungs. He spoke out again: "Why do we do this?" Then continuing to himself: build roads, ride over them, make holes, patch them, make more holes. It was like that for the whole village, everybody doing the same thing again and again, the women cooking and cleaning, the men repairing the maze of penning walls, hauling stones from the moor in their wagons, moving the animals from one pen to another, shearing the sheep, milking the cows. And he forever mending something for somebody, fixing loose tiles in the roofs, deepening the wells, sealing pipes.

"We never get anywhere," he said and tried to imagine where a car that odd could possibly take the man. Patrick pictured him at the end of the peninsula following the road out to the blue water's edge and sailing for a city where great towers soared toward the sun.

He worked for another hour, sitting cross-legged on the blacktop, picking out chunks one at a time, spitting phlegm into each hole before he tipped the pot of tar.

Then he saw the stranger walking in from the fields, not on the road, but taking a zigzag path back and forth among the scattering of large rocks, stepping from one to another as if playing a game in which his feet were not allowed to touch the earth. He wore baggy white coveralls and tan canvas shoes that laced up above the ankles. Over his shoulder was slung a cloth bag patterned with bright chalked designs. As the man came nearer, Patrick could hear tools clanging inside it.

"Car break down?" he said, disappointed that the man was not still traveling, farther and farther away from this place.

The man nodded, the bronzed skin of his head smooth and tight. For a moment Patrick thought he was very young, then saw the puckered flesh of his throat. "A car like that," the man said, "it was bound to happen."

The way he spoke surprised Patrick, soft and light, as if each word were a bubble that floated off the moment he let it loose. "Then why take it out there?" Patrick pointed toward a cluster of hills so distant they blurred into the clouds.

"That's how I discover where I should be."

Patrick blinked his puzzlement. "What?"

"Buy the cheapest car I can find that starts, point it in a direction, and drive until it won't run any more."

"Then?"

"I settle in where I am."

"For how long?"

"Until it's time to go someplace else."

"When's that?"

"When I get an idea about the way things should look here."

"It doesn't make sense," Patrick said, suddenly angry because he didn't understand and suspected the man was mocking him.

"I've come to make things different," the man said again as if that were an answer. He took a path behind the houses, and Patrick watched his loping strides until he was out of sight.

Patrick spent a long time cleaning the tar off his arms that evening, rubbing his skin with a kerosene rag and then lathering soap again and until his flesh stung. By the time he got to the tavern, it was crowded, the old men in black caps and suit coats lined on the bench against the wall watching the others with craggy, expressionless faces, the families sitting around the tables in the middle, children on their laps, the young lovers huddled in corners secretly touching each other.

As Patrick knew it would be, the conversation was about the stranger, and it struck him that was why he had delayed so long, because he didn't know what he would say. Everyone stopped when he entered the room. From behind the bar, Herbert slid him a glass already filled with brown liquid as if it had been waiting for him.

"We saw you talking to that man, Patrick," Edna Morris said, waving a cigarette, the little girl clinging to her shoulder, blonde and thin as her pale mother, staring wide-eyed at him as if he too had suddenly become a stranger. Long ago, before she married Arnie, Edna had sat tight against Patrick in those dark corners. He hadn't let himself remember in years, but now that she was staring right at him, he burned with blushing and quickly turned away.

"What did he tell you?" Arnie slid his chair back and stood over him.

"He's going to stay here," Patrick blurted. "For a while, anyhow."

The others gave out a murmur of dismay. Even the old men on the bench were shaking their heads.

"Now why would anybody want to do that?" Herbert said, both his hands gripping a tap.

"There's nothing here for him," Arnie said.

"There's nothing here for any of us." Mrs. Collins laughed, shaking her plump red face, though nobody laughed with her, not even her wizened husband sitting shrunken on the stool next to her. She had been a dear friend of Patrick's mother when his mother was alive, and he always felt that she was disappointed with him for turning out to be who he was.

In his mind Patrick rehearsed telling them: he buys old cars and drives them until they break down; that's his way of finding a place to make different. But he realized how foolish that would sound and worried that the others would blame him for saying something so ridiculous.

"I don't like it," Arnie insisted, slapping his hand against the bar top. The others grunted agreement, shifting uneasily in their seats.

"Well, we can't make him leave," Mrs. Collins said. "People are free to do what they want."

Patrick looked down at the floor planks, unwilling to meet the other's eyes.

Where was the man now? What was he up to? Everyone was talking at once. When all the thick speculation in that small, tight room began to smother him, Patrick pushed out the door and stood in the street gasping the cold air. He expected someone to follow him, a hand reaching from behind to grip his shoulder. But no one came, and he turned toward the creek bridge as if to walk until he vanished into the rocks.

Just before the bend, he saw a rush of sparks explode against the night, and seconds later heard the sizzle of embers. The stranger must have stirred his fire. Patrick imagined the man resting his head on the bright cloth pack, searching the black sky for a glow of starlight. He would cover himself with straw, drink goat's milk, eat boiled roots. That was all a man like him would need.

Early in the morning, Patrick, usually the first one to begin working, took the shovel from his shed and stepped out onto the street. Narrow streaks of orange dawn glowed from behind the clouds, the closest sign of sunshine he could remember in days. But the wind swirled a chill dampness through his coat.

The stranger was already standing on the green triangle of grass where the street widened between Herbert's tavern and the Vances' store. Still in the white coveralls, the bright bag on the ground beside him, he paced from the center to an edge of the triangle with long even steps, then back to the center and out to another edge, as if measuring. When he noticed Patrick, he nodded. Patrick returned a quick wave of his hand, wondering how many people were watching from behind the curtained windows.

"Who owns this land?" the man asked.

"What land?" Patrick said, not sure if he meant the village or the moor.

"This." The man pointed down at his feet, and Patrick saw he was talking about the small triangle.

He shrugged. "Nobody. All of us, I suppose."

"Who do I have to ask for permission to use it?"

"For what?"

"I want to build something."

"There?" Patrick shook his head. "It's too small for anything."

"Not for what I want to build."

"I don't know about permission," Patrick said. "When somebody wants to build a house or a barn, they just do it." Then he realized he probably had told the man something he shouldn't have, that everyone would be furious with him.

"Then why don't I just start and if anybody doesn't like it they'll tell me to stop."

"Maybe that's not such a good idea," Patrick said.

"We'll have to find out." The man began forcing thin sticks into the soft earth, evenly spaced, as if he had used a ruler.

Patrick rushed directly to the land behind Susan Crane's vegetable garden, digging furiously at the shrubbery that grew around the rocks, hacking at roots with the shovel blade, unable to cut through, finally beating the shovel against the stone and stinging his hands with a shock of pain. He dropped the handle and squeezed both hands under his armpits.

The sheep stopped to stare at him with their narrow black faces and quickly returned to nibbling at the grass. Now Patrick worked slowly and methodically, prying up the rocks one at a time and stacking them in a pile behind him, try to concentrate on guessing the crops Susan would plant in this new space. He didn't want to think what the stranger might be doing on the wedge of land. He was far enough from the village to see nothing or hear nothing. But he had forgotten to bring anything to eat or drink, and by the afternoon was so tired and thirsty he had to go back.

He took a roundabout path to his cottage that bypassed the village center, not wanting to see the changes the man had made, to have the others look at him as if he was to blame for the man's existence. Once inside he drank a quart of milk, then rubbed the cool glass across his face and down his neck. His first thought was to fall on the bed and sleep. But a clamor of voices rose from the center and he was drawn to the sound.

The people of the village were standing on both sides of the street, the Collinses, Herbert at the tavern door, the Vances by the front of their store, Edna Morris and her daughter with a group of the other small children huddled around them, three old men on a bench by the post office, people up and down the way, Arnie Morris apart from the rest, alone in the center of the road, face clenched and legs rooted.

Patrick looked for the stranger and finally saw him at the corner of the schoolhouse dragging a great rock behind him on a sheet of canvas, a thick rope tied through holes in the material and wrapped around his waist and shoulders. Patrick had never seen a canvas like that and wondered where the man had gotten it.

Dragging the rock was harsh work. Veins stood out on the man's bald head as he strained, and sweat poured down his face. The coveralls were filthy now, as if they had never been white. No one moved to help. Instead the people shrank back as he struggled past, grunting with each step he took. Eventually he came up to Arnie Morris and stopped, his chest heaving deep breaths. Arnie ground his bootheels down at the pavement and would not move.

Patrick was surprised at the size of Arnie; he had seen him every day of his life and never realized how big he was. Once when he was young, he had fantasized about fighting Arnie for Edna, and now he saw how foolish that would have been.

Arnie stared hard at the stranger and drew back an arm. Patrick could hear Edna gasp, but Arnie just brushed the hair back from his forehead and stepped aside. The man gave him a half smile and heaved at the canvas.

Patrick looked past him at the triangle and saw three other rocks just as large as the one the man was dragging. A dozen long metal pipes lay aligned on the grass. When the man got the canvas to the edge, he rolled the rock off beside the others, spread the canvas next to the pipes, and sprawled out full length, his chest heaving.

The people watched for a time until they saw that he was sleeping. One by one they looked at each other, turned, and went back into their houses. Patrick realized that he was the last one out on the street.

That evening he didn't go to the tavern, his body sorer than he could remember in years, as if he had been the one to move all those great rocks from the moor.

Patrick avoided the village the next morning even though he had promised Hilda Sayers to dig a trench and lay new pipes for drainage. Instead, still tired and aching despite a night of heavy sleep, he sat on a hillock among the sheep and studied the ewe Charlie Kimball had only half sheared the other day, irregular hanks of long hair alternating with patches of smooth white skin. It seemed unfair to the animal to make it look so freakish, half naked and vulnerable.

In late afternoon when he made himself go back, he saw the stranger had spaced the rocks on the triangle, three in one row and another angled away from them in an arrangement that made Patrick sense a plan. Now the man was drilling into the rock with a gas-powered machine that made an uneven sputtering sound as the long bit ground into the stone and sprayed grey chips. The man wore goggles that covered most of his face. Wide black streaks stained the front of his coveralls.

Not many people were watching at this time of the day, besides the children who stayed far back, just the old men, the Vances, the Collinses, and Edna Morris. Patrick looked for Arnie but only saw his rusted van in the alley beside Herbert's tavern, curtains drawn across the windows.

When the holes were drilled, the man picked up a length of pipe and slipped it deep inside one of them, stepping back to study it and then tamping it down. He put a pipe in each rock, but at varying depths, so that the exposed ends rose up at different levels. Then he capped one pipe, the shortest, with an elbow joint, screwed in another length at a right angle parallel to the ground, and swung it sideways until it touched one of the other standing pipes. For his canvas bag he removed a blowtorch, lit a blue flame, and welded the two pipes. He worked deliberately, pausing to step back and measure with his eyes. Eventually the pipes in the rocks were all connected by crosspieces.

The stranger drew spots on two of the crosspieces and reached a new pipe from one to the other, but it rolled away from the marked spots. "Would somebody help me?" he said.

Patrick felt Edna looking at him and made himself stare back at her. Their eyes locked as if each were daring the other to step forward. He could feel his muscles shuddering as if the decision to move would change his life. When Edna broke the contact, he saw Mrs. Collins already standing on the triangle holding an end of the pipe.

"Will it hurt?" She laughed boldly, but Patrick sensed that she was frightened. Her husband had gone into their house.

"It won't hurt and it won't feel good," the man said.

"Then I suppose I'm wasting my time," she said but pressed the pipe down onto his marking.

The stranger welded the other end firm and then the one Mrs. Collins had gripped. He picked up another length of pipe, and she helped him again until none remained loose on the ground. When he was finished, the four rocks were connected by a network of pipes that Patrick realized fanned out from the one apart to the row of three.

Arnie Morris appeared at the tavern door and shouted out, "What the hell's that supposed to be?"

"Not much as far as I can tell," Mrs. Collins shouted back.

The man gathered up his wrenches and drill, put the blowtorch back in the cloth bag, then walked out of the village. Patrick wondered what would happen if he followed but was unwilling to try.

———————————

That night Arnie, drunk in the tavern, tried to talk the others into storming out to the triangle and ripping those pipes apart. Edna wasn't there nor was Mrs. Collins and most of the women. The men cheered Arnie on, plotted strategy, but did nothing, and when Arnie collapsed open-mouthed, his face flat against the damp bar top, slipped away with quiet goodnights to Herbert.

———————————

Up at dawn, Patrick expected to see the stranger at work when he got to the street. But the man wasn't in the triangle. Curious, Patrick searched through the village, then gave up, wondering if the man had finished whatever he planned and left for good. He had just begun digging the trench for the Sayers when he spotted him walking past the pond with pieces of the green car hanging from ropes over his shoulder and tied to his waist—headlights, red lenses, a steering wheel, bumper guards, tail pipe. Over his head he carried the metal sheet of the hood.

His coveralls were ripped now, split down the center of the back, exposing muscled flesh. Patrick thought he was less tan than he had been on the first day, already losing his color in the sunless climate.

Patrick couldn't help speaking. "What's all that for?"

The man gave him a thin smile. "I knew what I'd use the moment I saw that car."

He's crazy, Patrick thought and gave all his attention to his digging.

Later, when he went back to the village center, he found the hood fixed to one of the crosspipes pointing straight up into the air. The headlights were embedded in the rocks at either end of the row and the red lenses in the middle one. The steering wheel rose above the fourth rock at the end of the tailpipe. But Patrick's greatest surprise was seeing Edna Morris's daughter sitting on the man's shoulders turning the steering wheel and laughing gleefully.

The street was filled with people, and when he spotted Edna in the group, he expected to hear her scream. But she was beside the Cranes pointing to her daughter and laughing. Arnie stood back by his house with his arms folded across his chest.

Patrick went to Mrs. Collins. "What's going on here?"

"We're all wondering what he'll do next."

When darkness fell, Patrick sat outside his cottage on an old barrel and watched the shapes of the people moving along the paths and gathering in front of the tavern. They were talking, but the breeze swallowed the sounds. Only Mrs. Collins' laughter rang clear.

He half wished she would come for him, reach out and lift him to his feet. It's over, she would say, forgotten, I forgive you. She had been so furious all those years ago, dragging him off the street into her living room the day after he had entered the tavern to find Arnie pressing Edna against the wall, she looking so young and fragile in the wrap of his broad arm. "Be someone!" Mrs. Collins had roared. "Do something!" "Look at me," he had told her, afraid he wouldn't be able to swallow his tears, stiff-armed, holding out palms as if to display the gangly awkwardness of his body, feeling the thick mat of hair tingling against his scalp. She had reached out and touched that hair. "Make youself good enough, Patrick." He hadn't been able to let himself fall against her.

More people gathered, and the murmur of voices rose until it was as loud as the wind. They probably were talking about the stranger, perhaps planning something. Nobody would have cared if he joined them. But he chose to stand apart. Once he had believed they were all talking about him, the target of Arnie's gloating. But he never heard Arnie say a word about him, as if he had never done anything worth comment.

Though he usually rode his bicycle to cover great distances, Patrick walked, following the road away from the village, out toward the pond and beyond. Over his shoulder he carried the steel bar he used for prying loose roots and rocks and long rusted spikes, occasionally swinging it out at the shrub tops and then pushing against the pavement as if it were a walking stick. When he started the sky was a soft grey above the brown hills at the horizon; for the first time in a week he could see behind them to the green cleft of a valley that always made him think of a woman. But as he walked the clouds darkened until he couldn't make out anything past the flat sprawl of rock and scrub grass and grazing sheep.

He hadn't admitted to himself where he was going; but now, out of sight of the village, he said, "I want to see his car," and wondered when he would come upon the hoodless ruin, how far the man had gotten past the village on the first day. Patrick didn't know what he would do when he saw it, why he had gone into his tool shed for the steel bar.

The rain began, first just a spray like mist in the wind and then a steady pelting. It soaked his hair and ran down beneath his collar. He imagined finding the car and sitting inside, being lifted from the ground by the swirl of a great storm and then coming down somewhere totally new, a place different from any he had ever imagined.

Then Patrick heard laughter, an excited roar. He ran to a curve in the road and saw almost everyone he knew, practically the whole village, swarming around the remains of that faded green automobile. They had come in trucks and carts and motorbikes, their vehicles scattered on the grass along the roadside.

The stranger's car was propped up on rocks by its axles, the four wheels loose and flat on the ground. Scrawny Mr. Collins was wrestling with the back seat, all by himself trying to slide it out the door, his wife with her arms wrapped around herself, shaking with delight.

The stranger was pointing down at the engine telling people what parts to remove, his coveralls tattered, the legs flapping in the wind and the top half hanging loose from his chest, sleeves knotted around his waist. Edna Morris stood close, listening, her arms pale white beside the golden flesh of his torso.

They all seemed oblivious of the rain, excited by their tasks. When Herbert saw Patrick, he shouted a greeting. "Just the man we need. Help me pry this door loose." He guided the steel rod between the hinge and the car frame, and the two of them heaved their weight against the lever until the metal snapped free.

When all the parts he wanted were spread out on the ground, the stranger walked among them as if committing each to memory. Then he supervised the loading into the carts and truck beds.

A caravan rode back to the village. Patrick started off walking beside it until Edna waved him onto the seat of Arnie's van. He squeezed in beside two young boys, and Edna's daughter sat on his lap touching a finger to his ears and chin and nose as if they were playing a game. Edna drove and Patrick wondered where Arnie was.

———————

In the village, they unloaded everything beside the triangle, and the stranger told them what to do. They wedged the back seat between two rocks, strung engine pieces to the crosspipes with wire—air filter, distributor, carburetor, spark plugs. When the man sliced the tires away, they stacked the wheels one atop the other and buried the four doors in the earth around them, so deep that only the windows showed.

Someone had gone for Patrick's shovel. He did most of the digging, all the time thinking, what's this for? But at nightfall, when the rain slowed to a drizzle, he stopped to look at the others, everyone filthy with mud but working as eagerly as he was, and he didn't care.

———————

The brightness glowed behind the morning haze, but a sheet of grey still blocked the sun. Before he went out Patrick gave himself a long wash, shaved closely, and put on clean clothes. The second he stepped into the street, he felt something was different and saw the thick wooden pole planted crooked in the triangle off to one side of the rocks, a sawed off scrub pine lashed to its top with hemp rope, tilting upward, above the green hood.

The others were rushing out of their houses with cries of surprise. From the way the stranger was standing in the center of the street looking up at the pole and shaking his head, Patrick knew at once he hadn't placed it there.

"It's wood," Mrs. Collins called out as if she had made a discovery. "Nothing else is wood."

"So what if it's wood?" Susan Crane yelled back.

"Is supposed to be rock and metal."

"There's no rules."

Patrick saw Arnie Morris leaning out of an upstairs window with a broad smile, as if he had just won a bet.

"Susan's right," Herbert said from the tavern door. "When you make something like that, you can do anything you want." The old men on the bench pinched their lips and nodded.

Two boys dragged a torn mattress across the street and leaned it against one of the rocks. The people cheered. Suddenly everybody was bringing something—an old dresser with broken drawers, flowers in clay pots, a bed post, a man's suit propped up on sticks like a scarecrow, a cracked bathtub. Arnie Morris carried three cans of paint, and he and Herbert smeared streaks of bright red and blue and yellow up, down, and across the rocks. Children tied ribbons to the pipes. The whole village was swarming over the triangle of ground, each person adding something different.

Patrick couldn't decide what he should do. It occurred to him that he could pour pools of tar over the grass patches. But as he turned toward his shed, he realized that the stranger wasn't there with all the others. He rushed through the paths behind the houses, opening unlocked doors, searching the outbuildings, until he was absolutely certain.

Patrick ran back to the street, ready to plunge into the crowd, shake people by the shoulders and tell them. But at the edge of the triangle he stopped, unsure that he could make anyone listen. He beckoned to Edna, called her name when she would not stop wrapping lamp wire around a pipe. She came to him, annoyed at the interruption. "What's the matter now?"

"He's gone."

"Who?"

Patrick didn't know what to call him. "The man who did all this."

"I know," she said. "The fool bought Arnie's old van. A wreck of a thing that won't get him from here to there."

"But look what's happening with him gone. It's not the way he made it."

"What's that matter? It's ours now."

She turned away, and Patrick walked backwards one step at a time, trying to understand the din of activity. But it just bewildered him. "I liked it better," he said aloud, "when he was making it by himself."

———————

Out in the moor, away from the village, Patrick stood and faced the distant hills, picturing the open sea beyond, imagining that the stranger had already crossed to a someplace new on the other side.

He pushed a stone loose from the top of a wall. It thudded to the earth and the sheep skittered away. Then, as if discovering the ground he walked on each day of his life, he removed stones deliberately, one by one, spreading them on the ground. With at least a hundred scattered at his feet, he grouped the largest in a base and began to lock the others into a pyramid that had nothing to do with penning animals. When he had used up the loose stones, Patrick paused and saw that it wasn't finished. He sensed a promise just past the reach of his fingertips, and his face opened into a smile. He had no idea what he was making but knew this land contained all the rock he would ever need.

Walter Cummins has published five previous short story collections—*Witness, Where We Live, Local Music, The End of the Circle,* and *The Lost Ones.* More than 100 of his stories, as well as memoirs, essays, and reviews, have appeared in magazines such as *Kansas Quarterly, Virginia Quarterly Review, New Letters, Under the Sun, Arts & Letters, Confrontation, Bellevue Literary Review, Connecticut Review, The Laurel Review, Other Voices, Georgetown Review, Contrary, Sonora Review, Abiko Quarterly, Weber Studies, Midwest Quarterly, West Branch, South Carolina Review, Crosscurrents, Crescent Review, The MacGuffin,* in book collections, and on the Web. With Thomas E. Kennedy, he is co-publisher of Serving House Books, an outlet for novels, memoirs, and story, poetry, and essay collections. For more than twenty years, he was editor of *The Literary Review.* He teaches in Fairleigh Dickinson University's MFA in Creative Writing and MA in Creative Writing and Literature programs.